Don't tell all your business!

Childhood Stories by
Timothy Allen

*To my most wonderful friend, Veinta!
love always,*

Timothy Allen

For all the cousins, the ones who have passed, and the ones that still remain.

Contents

Foreword

Lick Skillet, Black Cat and Toney are the names of communities that are nestled in the vertices of what I fondly call the Bermuda Triangle of Alabama. It is not an area where people or vehicles have been lost or disappeared, although there was the wagon and horses that were never found mentioned in the book. Rather than people or things in this place, it is stories that seem to either have been lost or became so convoluted with the passage of time that not even a vestige of truth could be found in them. Strange things do seem to have happened there, especially where my family is concerned. Looking back, we could have easily appeared from a strange mist or fog. We could have arisen from the ground or descended from an unidentifiable silver object in the sky. But more than the powers that existed in the Triangle and that reeked havoc with us, it was my grandmother and her generation that seemed to have been responsible for what happened to the stories.

I could always tell when my grandmother became uneasy at an unfavorable story being told, or unflattering information being shared. Her back would straighten, a sudden intake of breath along with a clicking of her teeth would ensue, quickly followed by her words of warning, "Don't tell all your business!" If such stories or information were to be shared after that, it would have to be in private and well beyond her hearing range. Even then, we would all shake a bit from the fear that she would somehow find out. As a result, some stories were forbidden for so long that they died away along with the family members involved or those that knew all the details. Others were lost in their retelling as facts became less firm and exaggerations seemed to bloom like a bed of daisies.

I thought long and hard about my grandmother's admonition before writing these stories. I kept reminding myself that I was one of her favorites, and as such, wouldn't suffer from an inordinate amount of her wrath. So far, I haven't felt a cold hand on my shoulder nor heard a discordant clicking sound in a sudden gust of wind. I hope that I at least made her chuckle with some of the stories. With the more serious ones, I can only pray she understands that the telling was part of a journey I had to take.

For those who wish to write their family stories, I do offer some advice. Among the many good and heart-warming things you find, there are also hard truths and overwhelming rushes of sadness when you least expect them, so be prepared. There were times when I openly laughed as I wrote. There were other times when I had to stop before I began to sob. It is difficult to revisit your childhood and not return with some of the baggage you thought you had left behind.

These stories are as accurate as I could make them. Some are compilations of events that took place over time and molded to fit into a single day. Others happened in the time line in which I wrote them. If I wasn't sure about some of them, I conferred with my cousins and my brother. It was a good experience for my brother and me. I called him numerous times for confirmation of things the way I remembered them. Sometimes, he concurred and other times he sent me in a completely different direction. When we talked, it was almost as if we were that age again. It reminded me to be thankful for him. He is a blessing in my life as are the many cousins we grew up with.

I'm not sure about my grandmother and her generation's approach to hide the bad things. Those secrets and the things we weren't allowed to speak about only became bigger and scarier as time passed. When I finally opened those many cans of worms, I did find unsettling things. But in the end, they were just things, things that somehow happened, good and bad. There were family members who made bad choices or had dark sides. When the stories shined light on them, it revealed a lot about how and why my brothers, cousins and I evolved. There seems to be a reason for our many neuroses and insecurities. It is information we should have always had.

Finally, a friend shared with me how one author explained writing stories. He said that writers really write for themselves. It makes them complete and if someone else enjoys what they have written, it is an added blessing. These stories I offer have helped me find my center again. I tried not to offend anyone in their telling. If I did I am sorry, not for the stories, but for the discomfort they might bring. For those that find memories of their own childhoods, derive lessons from the darker stories or simply chuckle or shed a tear, you have blessed me beyond what I deserve.

The Luckless Family

I don't know how other families gauge luck. I mean I know they have rabbit's feet or four leaf clovers or an occasional newly found penny, heads up of course, but it's still hard for me to fathom it all. I grew up in a family in which we were taught at an early age that good luck was never to be ours. Occasional flukes of good fortune were in no way to be confused with luck. And those flukes, we learned, were always later to be followed by misfortune or catastrophes. We were not led easily into this belief or mindset. My father could back every claim he made with hard evidence. So when my uncle would profit from selling land that lay next to my father's that in the end lost money, we had already learned to shrug our shoulders and continue with our lives. My father had put it all succinctly to my brothers and me one day with the words, "You know you're never meant to have nothing, and if you do, something will happen to take it away." My father actually spoke well, and now I think that the double negative was also meant to add weight to his words. Those words indeed proved heavy for my brothers and me. We should have had them embossed on tee shirts since they directed the majority of our lives, and somehow my brothers and I, in a variety of ways, proved the adage to be true again and again.

We weren't really obvious in our secret knowledge. I mean, it wasn't as if we walked around with black clouds over our heads. The letter "L" was not tattooed on our foreheads. We didn't dress like Goths. Outwardly, we really appeared quite normal, as normal as any kids who had been raised in an area between communities named Lick Skillet and Black Cat. And no, the name "Black Cat" did not refer to a haven for the luckless. In those days community names were chosen for the simplest of reasons. Somebody probably owned a black cat and said, "Hey. I have an idea." Anyway, people who knew us all along would never have guessed that we were luckless. We were fairly popular in school and my parents were well thought of. Actually, most people probably would have argued against even the possibility that we were luckless. But it was enough that my family knew. Though we didn't realize it, our father had given us the perfect out in life, the unbreakable alibi, a way to explain any of our stupidities, and there were many for all three brothers.

So, two or three failed marriages later for my brothers and countless unsuccessful relationships for me, I guess it was inevitable that luck would hit us all smack dab in the face. In the cosmic scheme of things, one might argue that sooner or later something good had to happen, you know luck of the draw, happenstance, being at the right place at the right time or stumbling on to a good thing. No matter, we would have still viewed it with learned suspicion and even perhaps found ways to cause it to sour had it not been for the way it appeared. Who in even their wildest imaginations could ever predict that an aging Rottweiler would appear one day at the edge of a yard and bring with him what was undeniably in the end good fortune that could not be trifled away? But that is exactly what happened. It was like a letter that had been lost in the mail for years finally finding its intended destination. Luck, or some facsimile of it, found us and made itself at home, somewhat like a cactus in the desert.

Boscoe, the Rottweiler, first appeared in the corner of my parent's side yard when they in their seventies were once again planting a garden. They had grown up in an era when everyone had a garden and to them I guess it represented more than what it produced. It also seemed to represent a perpetual usefulness in their lives. This they did not pass on to my brothers and me. Growing up, we knew the signs of garden planting, or tending, or picking and had learned to conveniently be occupied. Our favorite escape was homework. "We'd love to help if it wasn't for these crazy summer assignments we have to complete for school, you know, like reading "War and Peace." My parents were always too involved with the task at hand to question the absurdity of our excuses. Anyway, as my mother and my dad were working in the garden that day, one of them, I don't know which, and I'm sure they even argued the point, looked up and saw their neighbor's Rottweiler lying there about one hundred feet away. He made no sound and no movement toward either one of them, so they continued with their work, occasionally checking to make sure that he had not shortened the distance between them. Being luckless did not mean one had to be reckless.

It took several days for my parents and Boscoe to surmise that there was no threat, at least no physical threat. Boscoe's canine sense could not have provided him with the knowledge that he was aligning with a luckless family. My parents could not have suspected that they were welcoming in anything more than a four-legged companion. So Boscoe edged closer, and my dad finally walked over and petted him. The petting led to food offerings. and just as Hansel and Gretel were lured to the witch's house, Boscoe made his gradual move to the back patio and then to the porch of my parent's home, not to be fattened for cooking, which would have indeed been unlucky, but to become a member of the family. He stayed there daily as long as my parents were at home, returning in the evenings after my mom and dad settled in for the night to his own home across the yard.

My parents had always been tolerant and generally fond of pets. With three sons growing up in the country, it was a given there would be dogs and an occasional cat. It wasn't that we were luckless with animals. Maybe the animals became luckless from association. We grew up in a time and place when the only medical assistance for animals was the yearly rabies shots always given at specified locations in the area such as a store or the post office. If one of our pets got sick beyond whatever the purple medicine purchased at the local hardware store could be applied to as a cure, they were out of luck. My brothers and I weren't aware for the most part of how they disappeared. One day they were there, followed by a night of muted parent conferences, and then the next day they were gone. We never had time to really grieve for any of them, because in the country there was always an abundance of animals without homes or new litters that had to be dispersed, so replacements seemed to appear almost immediately.

After my brothers and I left home, I can remember my parents only having two pets, both cats. They really were my dad's cats and they bonded to the point that I guess my dad forgot for a brief time that we were never meant to have nothing. Each cat would follow him around or lie in his lap or at his feet. He talked to them and sang to them and on occasion played his French harp. Both came to untimely ends. If my dad had somehow begun to question his philosophy regarding luck, those cats' deaths squelched such perusals. He was so devastated by both deaths that he swore that he would never own another animal, and once again he was assured that as a family we were to always remain in an elite group in which luck was perpetually absent.

Boscoe circumvented my dad's adamant stance through technicalities. After all, he wasn't really their pet. Also, he was such a behemoth, the possibilities of something happening to him seemed slim to none.

So over a period of months, he became a fixture at my parents' house. When any family member visited, there was Boscoe either snoozing on the back porch, by the garden watching my parents work, following my mother while she rode the riding lawn mower as if she were in a stock car race or splayed on his back in the yard exhibiting his jewels, as my dad was quick to point out while shaking his head and chuckling.

At this point Boscoe had not really altered our failure at finding luck. My nieces and nephews continued to falter in relationships. One of my brothers not only changed women like his socks, but began numbing the results of his bad choices with excessive drinking. My parents continued to look at each other with their self-assured knowledge that they could have been something more had it not been for the other, perhaps allowing the luckless legacy to have been responsible for them even being together. He did, however, change our focus somewhat. If we centered our attention on him, we could somehow forget for brief periods that we were not meant to have nothing.

Unfortunately for Boscoe, he too finally succumbed to the inevitable family curse. Lumps on his left front leg turned out to be cancerous. In order to contain the cancer, they had to remove the entire leg. After his surgery my family did not see him for days as he remained home with his owners recuperating. We really did not expect to see him again. After all, there was no way possible that this huge Rottweiler could support his weight on three legs much less maneuver any significant distance. My parents were grief stricken of course, and a pall of sadness and reaffirmation of the absence of luck seemed to settle over every family gathering.

Then one day when I pulled in my parents' driveway for the customary Sunday dinner, there on the back porch was Boscoe, three-legged and happy, rolling over for me to rub his belly. He had been able to traverse the three hundred yards from his house to my parents' home and even climb the back steps to their porch. The difference in my parents registered not only in their faces, but in the way they interacted with each other. The difference in the family was like a fog rolling out leaving a lightness of spirit. This had to be how being lucky felt, we surmised, though no one voiced it. Putting it into words might have jinxed it in some way and we were not strong enough in the possibilities that were offered in any way to challenge it.

As we sat and ate our dinners for months after that, my father would go to the back door and talk to Boscoe who resided on the porch just beyond. He would ask Boscoe if he wanted him to sing and Boscoe would respond with the low guttural sounds one would expect from a dog his size. My dad would sing and Boscoe would sing too, in his own way. Sometimes, my dad played his French harp like he used to do with his cats. Other times, they would simply converse as one old friend to another. Boscoe could have been no closer to being a member of our family had he been sitting at the dinner table.

I think there was a purpose to Boscoe's return beyond forcing us to reexamine our lifelong obsession with how unlucky we always were. After my dad's prognosis of cancer, his health began to deteriorate rapidly. Through all the horrifying treatments and symptoms he suffered, Boscoe was always there when he got home. Dad spent more and more of his time sitting on the back patio, absent of energy and a decreasing will to fight it anymore. Boscoe was always there lying at his feet even when my dad slept, which had now become most of the time.

When my dad died, Boscoe initially would look for him. He would wait by the door for conversations or music. Finally, as if he had resolved that he wouldn't return, he turned his attentions to my mother. I think Boscoe knew that she needed him. As he aged, it took him longer and longer to lumber the distance from his house to my mother's. Some days, you could see him resting halfway. But eventually he always made it. Watching him climb the steps was painful and my mother worried that he would fall and hurt himself. So she would try to feed and water him out on the level yard, placing his food so that he wouldn't have to move to get it. Still we would find him on the porch as if that was the place he was meant to be.

I remember the lunch when just my mother and I sat at the table and she told me she didn't think she could handle it if Boscoe died on her porch. She was to be spared that sadness. Arthritis or the cancer or maybe a bit of both had finally claimed him. His owners took him to the vet who gave him a shot to ease the pain. He was no longer able to walk the distance to my mother's. His owners took him inside their house to make him more comfortable. He lasted only days after that.

When my father died, I was devastated, but somehow I don't think I ever grieved. As long as there was Boscoe on the back porch, or in the yard or even lumbering over to see me when my car pulled in the driveway, I still sensed that my father was there. When Boscoe died he didn't just take away a dog I had grown to love, he also took away my father's soft cajoling voice, the sound of his singing, the strange and sometimes discordant sounds of his French harp, and left in its place the knowledge that he and my father would not return.

What this 100-pound three-legged dog taught my family and me was that luck is not something one has or doesn't. It is just a thing. It doesn't control people's lives nor intervene on a random basis to affect what happens one way or another. It really has nothing to do with outcomes, whether they are considered windfalls or catastrophes. I do grant that luck exists, but not in the way my father always taught me. If you happen to find a four leaf clover, that is indeed lucky, as it is a rarity of nature. There is nothing lucky about a rabbit's foot. Just ask all the three-legged rabbits. These days I am more inclined to interject the word blessed, where I had been taught to use the word luck. I am most certainly blessed to have my family and friends. I was blessed to have my father for so many years. I was blessed by the opportunity to know Boscoe and when I find a penny on the street, heads up of course, I am blessed to have found it. In a way, I guess I am also lucky, lucky to have one more penny in my pocket.

Serpents in Skillet

When I was three or four my family and I lived with my father's father, Daddy Jim, in the heart of Lick Skillet, Alabama. It was an economical thing, as was everything during that period of time. My father had finally acquired a good job on Redstone Arsenal and we were waiting on the completion of a house my parents were building on land they had purchased from my mother's family.

Daddy Jim owned a small farm with a four room house, a barn and an outhouse. It is hard to imagine that my mother, father, two older brothers and I were a comfortable fit in this setting. But this was during a time when people made do with what they had or didn't have. What Daddy Jim didn't have was a lot of space or money. What he did have was a big heart and he would have done anything to help out his youngest son's family to find a better path in life.

My father was a late life baby. I think Daddy Jim was in his sixties when he was born and married to his fourth wife. It would have been his fifth, if you count the one he married and then left by pretending to go to the smoking car at the back of the train, only to leave a trail of smoke as he jumped to freedom. Come to think of it, he might have been the first E-cigarette, since he didn't smoke, but vanished like a vapor, while his new bride continued north on the train.

Lest one think that my grandfather was an unfaithful cad, in truth, he outlived his other three wives, after they had birthed and raised families. Of course, there is a family living somewhere up north who would contradict this belief as they recount tales of the one who got away. My father and his sister were born to his last wife, whom he also outlived.

Being in the last lot might explain Daddy Jim's generosity to my dad and our family. My father, who seemed to have a very complicated relationship with my grandfather, would attribute it all to redemption. In Daddy Jim's life, nothing came before his religious beliefs. He was so deeply rooted in his convictions that my father and his younger sister were always relegated secondary roles. Somehow, in my dad's mind, this equated to never being good enough in anything he did or said to be a priority in his father's eyes. Whatever the reason, there we were for more than a year smack dab in the middle of the Skillet.

There were two things I remember most about Daddy Jim while we lived there. First, he always seemed to be sitting in his favorite chair reading his Bible. In my mind, I can picture him there with his white hair, wearing wire-framed reading glasses, immersed in the word of God. Still, I don't remember him ever being cross with me for interrupting his time with the Lord. What I got from him was the purest love you can imagine, perhaps the type of love he was unable to give my father. And with it came the second thing I remember most. He had an old cigar box where he kept all manner of things he had found, a piece of a watchband, cuff links that had lost their mates, a marble found in the field, tiny pebbles that were worn to a delicious smoothness, the cap of an acorn, old buttons and a multitude of other things that had simply caught his eye. He would sit me in his lap and open the box and let me choose whatever I wanted. It was like Christmas every day.

There were other things that lived on the farm besides my family that mostly impacted my uncle and middle brother. Uncle Dean was not really my uncle. He was a double first cousin or a cousin once removed or something very complicated when looking at lineage. He was almost removed as you will shortly see, so that part is true. However, our true family ties still mystify me to this day. You see, when my grandfather married one of his wives, they both had children from previous marriages. One of each of their children then married and in turn had children. It was like a limb was grafted onto the family tree. To this day I am at a loss to discern whether some of my relatives are half or fourth or maybe even three quarters cousins. We would make for a good fraction lesson. And all those nuts that fall from the tree? I always look to see if any of them bear a strong family resemblance.

Anyway, back to the other things that lived on the farm. Besides the rats and other assorted critters that lived and roamed the farm, there were also snakes. I don't guess they were poisonous as both my brother and uncle would be dead. Come to think of it, they could have been serpents that slithered right out of Daddy Jim's Bible. But we weren't in the desert and there were no relatives named Moses, at least that I know of. And they didn't seem to congregate around an apple tree, if snakes really do ever congregate. Daddy Jim would have said that they do, especially at all the other churches in the area excluding the Church of God he attended. Regardless of where they came from, they were there. And my brother and uncle encountered them in very different ways.

For my Uncle Dean, it all began with the call of nature. With magazine or newspaper under his arm and perhaps a whistle flowing forth from his lips, he strode across the backyard to the outhouse. He was going to do some serious business as it would have been called back then. I don't think taking a dump had been coined yet and the sh-t word if uttered elsewhere, was certainly not used at my grandfather's house. So my uncle assumed his customary position on the wooden throne and proceeded to hang the imaginary closed for business sign on the door that purported large gaps to ensure proper ventilation. I don't know how far he had gotten into the article he was reading or whether he found it interesting or not. I assume if you didn't like what you were reading; it became part of the finishing up process. But, as he sat there disposing of the turnip greens my grandmother had cooked for supper the night before (always good for regularity according to all older members of the family) he felt a slight movement against his feet. When he peered over his reading material he saw a large snake slithering between his feet and toward the door. He set a new world's record for the long jump or at least a record in the Lick Skillet community. He leapt through the door with his pants and underwear still bunched around his ankles, reading material still in his hands and landed a good six yards beyond the outhouse. From that point the story becomes murky. Did he do a crazy duck walk to put more distance between him and the snake? Had another batch of processed turnip greens been excreted? Did he complete the required hygienic procedures? All we know is he survived, and a very shaky snake as well as my uncle probably required psychiatric help.

My middle brother, who would have been eight or nine at the time, was less fortunate than my uncle. I guess there were ways he was actually more fortunate. He wasn't caught in the middle of making some serious deposits in the family outhouse. He also didn't have his britches down around his ankles with his family jewels displayed to the world. But if asked, I'm sure he would have chosen those things over his actual encounter. You see, since it was a working farm, my two older brothers had daily chores to do. It was my middle brother's job to gather the eggs each morning. So, with basket in hand he would traverse the distance from the house to the barn. He probably skipped, as he was a good-natured and happy lad. Maybe he even sang some childhood ditty as he went. It was almost like a fairy tale. You know, innocent child heading into a dark place to meet Satan's spawn. In the barn, the chickens roosted and laid their eggs in wooden bins that had been built on a wall in the side of one of the stalls. They were high enough off the ground to prevent egg-eating critters from reaching them. So, in order for my brother to reach them, he had to stand on his tippy toes and stretch his arms to their fullest extent. He would feel inside each bin until he found the eggs and then place them gently into the basket. It was business as usual that morning until he reached the last bin. With a basket filled with fresh eggs hanging on one hand, he stretched the free hand up and into the bin. What he grabbed hold of however, was not an egg, but the recently filled scaly, slimy, cold midsection of a chicken snake. He, like my uncle, also set a world's record that day. He was a blur, much like a superhero with the gift of speed. One minute he was in the barn and the next he was on the porch screaming for a sweet chariot to take him home to heaven. My oldest brother and I didn't see much of him that day. He disappeared into a world where only he and my mother resided. It is a miracle he didn't end up with a lifelong stutter. Come to think of it, he was never really good at Easter egg hunts after that. I also remember that we didn't have eggs for breakfast that morning and no one complained. If we had, my mother would have burned us to a heap of ashes with one of her deadly laser looks.

My brother and uncle both survived, though probably bearing deep-seated scars from close encounters with the serpents. As for the rest of us, when the new house was completed, we left Lick Skillet to live in the Toney community on the same road as my mother's parents. We left Daddy Jim still reading his Bible in the little house on his farm. Just as my brother was changed by the snake, I also was shaped by my time there. Because of my grandfather, I am obsessed with wooden and metal boxes. I have them all over my house, big ones, little ones, some ornate and others so plain they would catch no one's attention but my own. I am also entranced by mismatched things that I find. If you open a drawer in my desk, you'll most likely find a small wooden ball, one leg from a plastic cowboy, old buttons, special marbles from sets that were lost, pieces of key chains, a cuff link or two, and countless items that have lost purpose other than to make me smile when I see them. And along the way, we all encounter serpents, whether they are the slithering kind or standing on two feet. All we can really hope for in the end is that they never catch us with our pants down.

Ain't Promise Ain't Sure

S ome stories never belong to you. They may be about you, and you may even be the main character, but they truly always belong to the teller. This story belonged to my dad. It is his numerous times telling it that firmly affixed it in my head. I was too young to remember many of the details of what happened then, including this story. Unfortunately, I seem to have many gaps of memory about much of my early childhood. There are images that appear from time to time, but they are murky at best. Sometimes my middle brother can confirm, deny or clarify them for me. After he is gone, I guess they will pass from murky to opaque and then be lost for good.

When my dad told this story, his face would light up. A huge smile would appear, and for the telling he would actually remove the hand that seemed to perpetually block his face. It was as if the shyness that dogged him had no place for a bit. Maybe, the story came more from his heart than his head, and that in itself was enough to stifle the insecurities he had grown up with. Whatever the reason, with hands in his lap or on the arm rests of his chair, he would look at me before he began the tale. In that look he conveyed both love and pride. In it I saw the importance of the story to him. It was something rare and special. It only belonged to him and me and one other, Ed Malone, who was his good friend.

There are some things you should know about Ed Malone and me that impact his story. I was somewhere between three and four years old. I had blonde hair that was so light it was almost the color of cotton. As a result, some people, especially Ed Malone, called me Cottontop. I had large brown eyes, one of which had nerve damage that greatly impaired its movement. The other eye compensated by moving too freely which often gave me the appearance of being cross eyed. I had an unusually high level of acid in my mouth which was deteriorating my baby teeth. This would be rectified a year later with all my teeth being covered with silver caps to preserve them. So, my smiles were all closed-lipped, which along with my chubby face made me look impish. Unlike my dad, I was never shy. I never hid behind a leg or the skirt of a dress. I was quite the opposite in fact. I seemed to want to please people from the word go, a trait that as I got older would prove to be both a blessing and a curse.

As for Ed Malone, he was a successful business man in Lick Skillet where we lived at the time. Lick Skillet was not really a town. It was more of a small community that happened to evolve as people started settling in close proximity to each other. Its true name was New Sharon, as was the name of the elementary school that operated there in the early years. There was no post office. It was comprised mainly, other than the school, of a couple of small stores, a cotton gin that was close by, and two churches, one of which was the Church of God, my grandfather's church. There are mixed opinions of where the nickname Lick Skillet came from. One story is that the people there were so poor that they had to swab their bread in the grease left in the skillet after cooking, or as they called it, lick the skillet. Another explanation involved an altercation at one of the stores. It seems an unruly customer had to be licked with a skillet, or hit in the head with one, to bring him to his better senses. Either story seems plausible to me. Perhaps both happened, giving double meaning to the name. And then again, maybe neither is true. What if someone had left a skillet out on the stove and their cat gave it a good cleaning? They would tell their neighbor, who would tell his neighbor and so on, until a most unusual name is born.

Ed Malone owned both a store and a cotton gin. He was a few years older than my dad and had known him long before he joined the army. He probably knew my dad better than anyone, even my mother. It was a given that they would be good friends. They both possessed good hearts and were generous and friendly by nature. They were different in that my dad was generally soft spoken, where Ed was loud and boisterous. Perhaps even that served their friendship, with Daddy tempering Ed's outspokenness and Ed encouraging my dad to speak up more.

Ed's store was typical of the country stores at the time, with gas pumps out front and an interior filled with just about anything anyone could need or want without having to drive to the closest city. There were glass display cases on both sides of the center aisle and behind them shelves that rose up the walls almost to the ceiling. You could find anything from hardware and basic car parts to fresh produce grown on the small farms in the area. There was a case for watches and jewelry. There was an aisle just for canned goods and another for pots and pans or other kitchen gadgets. All of these cases and shelves were set on a wooden floor that had sustained spills from every imaginable liquid and the scuffing from countless shoes.

In those times, shoes wore down more quickly as people were too busy simply trying to get by to worry about picking up their feet.

Sometimes the weight of what they carried made the soles of their shoes dig even deeper into the wood. It was a floor to be swept, not polished. In a way that is probably a good description of Ed. In his tan work clothes with his hat pulled down over his brow and the cigarette that seemed to perpetually dangle from his bottom lip, he could be cleaned up a bit, but never polished. He was a full-of-life country boy that never forgot what hardship was like. There is no telling how many families he helped during hard times by either extending them credit, or forgiving debts they couldn't pay. Sometimes, people stopped by his store only to visit or talk. For everyone who came to the store he had a smile, a laugh, a pat on the back, and at times a kind ear with the appropriate head-nodding for the saddest of stories he would hear. Other than my grandfather, Daddy Jim, it is Ed Malone I remember the most from living in the Skillet.

As for the story, we would all be sitting at the dinner table after a big meal or in lawn chairs in someone's backyard after a cookout. Sometimes, we would be out on the back patio with a slight breeze keeping the worst of the heat at bay. My dad would scan those assembled, look at me, and the story would begin. "Have I told y'all the story about Timbo and Ed Malone's store when we lived in Skillet?" Everyone would pause any conversation and look at him. Even the ones that had heard it time and time again would shake their heads no. His voice was soft, cajoling and at that moment full of merriment. "Old Timbo was a little past three years old and had my friend Ed who owned the store on the corner wrapped around his chubby little finger. If he was with me at the store, Ed would pat him on the head, pick him up if the store wasn't too busy and always give him something, usually candy, but sometimes a small toy. It was the craziest thing. All three boys could be with me, and though he would charge the older two for the candy or drink they wanted, he never charged Timbo. He would give Timbo whatever he had chosen while grinning so big you'd think the cigarette was going to drop from his mouth and say, 'No charge for Cottontop.' If I came without him, Ed would look out the front store window asking where he was. If I tried leaving him in the car, Ed would take something out to him.

"I started thinking that Ed was being too generous to him. The only thing I knew to do was to try and sneak out of the house, especially if I was heading to the store. Well, that didn't work with old Timbo. No sooner would I have the front door half-opened than he would appear, fast as a jackrabbit, with his little hand grabbing and tugging on the leg of my pants. I knew looking down at him was a risk, but I decided to start out on solid ground. 'Son, I'm only going for gas and I'll be right back.' But with his little head with the white hair shooting in all directions tilted back so that his brown eyes could focus on me with unwavering determination, I knew I would have to shift my approach. 'Alright you can go, but under one condition. You have to promise me you won't ask or beg for anything while we're there.'

'I promise,' he would offer while never shifting his eyes from mine. 'Are you sure you can keep that promise once we get there?' I was skeptical at best. 'I sure!' He said with what I thought was great conviction. 'Okay then.' I loaded him in the car. He stood as close to me as he could while we drove to the store. He didn't seem to be looking anywhere, but straight ahead to where the store was. I was already wondering how long his resolve would last."

"When Ed came out to pump the gas, he beamed when he saw his partner in crime inside. 'There's my friend, Cottontop. What's up little buddy?' Timbo presented the biggest closed-lipped smile he could offer and shrugged his shoulders. When the two of us followed Ed into the store, I knew the true test was ahead. You see, the register rested on the top of a glass case that housed all the candy. As I paid, I could see Timbo's eyes scouring the case at breakneck speed while his little brain was looking for some loophole in the deal he had made. Sure enough, as Ed was giving me my change, there was a tug on my pants. When I looked down, there was his face with all resolve either forgotten or tossed aside.

'Can I have just one gumball?' was what he asked.

"I was doing a better job of trying not to smile than Ed. I said to him as sternly as I could muster, 'Now, son, our deal was that you promised not to ask for anything and you told me you were sure you could keep that promise.'

"Now, I want you to know I don't think he was being defiant. I think he had reached the conclusion that there was only one way he could fix the problem he faced. He looked at Ed and then looked at me and pronounced with even more conviction that he showed when we made the deal, 'Ain't promise, ain't sure!'

"Ed was laughing so hard he had to take the cigarette from his mouth. It took every ounce of resolve I had not to join him. Before I was forced to make an adult decision as how to respond, Ed offered, 'Jake, I think I know how we can fix this. You don't want Cottontop to get something for nothing. So, here's what we'll do. If Cottontop will dance for me, he can have anything in the store he wants.' Well it's a given that all of you, or most of you at least, know Timbo can dance. But you probably don't know he was pretty much dancing as soon as he could walk. Lord only knows where he learned it, or if he even learned it at all. Maybe he was born with it. Regardless, it didn't matter where he was or what everybody else was doing, and even if there wasn't music playing within a mile of him, he would start shuffling his little feet and do a little jig, so to speak. Ed had seen him do this a time or two in the parking lot of the store, so it really wasn't an unusual request for him to make. As if to close the transaction, Timbo simply nodded his head, and then on the floor in front of the display case with all the candy, he began to shuffle his feet and move his arms. He would tap and kick and occasionally spin. It was like he had a song playing in his head, and whatever it was, he danced to its rhythm. Either the song was long or he felt an obligation to Ed to give a stellar performance, because his little jig lasted for several minutes. The whole time both Ed and I were laughing and clapping. Then, as if the last note of the song sounded, he stopped, looked up at Ed and smiled the biggest most impish closed-lipped smile he could offer."

My dad would usually pause at this point, maybe because he needed to gather himself a bit from his chuckling that seemed to throw off the cadence of his story. He would take a moment to scan his listeners and then look at me with the biggest smile. I would smile back with the same closed-lipped smile that I must have presented back then. He would shake his head and continue the story. "When Ed finally stopped clapping and laughing, and for one of the few times I remember without a cigarette in his mouth, he looked at Timbo and said, 'A deal's a deal. Pick out anything you want.' Now I assumed he would choose the gumball he had initially asked for. But then he paused, looked at Ed and asked, 'Anything?' I'll have to admit I began to worry just a little bit. Timbo surveyed the candy in the display case and then began walking down the aisles with his brown eyes scanning all the shelves from floor to ceiling. He stopped and looked in the jewelry case which made me even more nervous, because I knew I would have to tell him no. He pretty much wandered through the entire store before he stopped in the area where Ed had the fresh produce displayed. He looked at me and then at Ed and pointed to the largest watermelon in the crate of melons. I have never been so relieved. Ed said, 'Is that what you want, Cottontop?' and Timbo nodded his head in the affirmative. 'It's yours.' Ed lifted him off the floor to carry him to the door while I carried the melon.

"I don't remember saying too much to Timbo on our way home. I was too busy either chuckling or trying to remember every detail so I could tell his mother, brothers and my father the story. I relayed it all at the supper table that night. I think I told it more than once at my father's request. And when supper was finished, we went out on the front porch and ate Timbo's prize watermelon for dessert."

At this point, my dad would grow quiet, as if he were replaying it all in his mind. He would chuckle and smile and repeat the phrases, "I promise, I sure," and "Ain't promise, ain't sure," more to himself than to the others around him. Those that heard his story were also laughing and most often looking at me to see if I was embarrassed by it. No matter how many times I heard him tell it, I was never embarrassed. I always felt an immense sense of pride from him and an undeniable and unconditional love.

Though this was always my dad's story to tell, the joy and amusement that came from it belonged to us both. In the twelve years he has been gone, I have tried my best to do things that would make him proud. But the older I get, I seem to gravitate more and more to making dubious decisions. When this happens, I like to look toward the sky and intone, "Ain't promise, ain't sure." I like to think he is watching, listening, shaking his head and chuckling. With the same affirmation he always offered me, he removes the hand that covers part of his face and says, "That Timbo, you just never know."

Quelling The Demons of Crazy

I t was a small house, larger than a playhouse and much smaller than a typical house. It would have fit into what we now see as being the new rage of tiny homes, the ones people build or buy to downsize in an exaggerated way to simplify their lives. But then, it served a much different purpose. It was surrounded by a chain link fence, one that was much taller than the ones erected to establish boundaries, protect kids from busy streets, or to give pets a safe place to wander outside the house. This fence more closely resembled those that enclosed a business with outdoor goods. It could have been a prison fence had the top consisted of barbed wire or the thin razor wire that slices at the slightest touch. The house and the fence were shaded by large trees in the spring and summer. In late fall and winter the bare limbs cast fingerlike shadows over it as if a giant hand was holding it in place. I remember these things about the tiny house because it was located to the side of a road my family and I traveled many times on our way to the city from our grandfather's home in Lick Skillet. We saw it as we headed out and there it would be again when we returned home.

One would think that my brothers or I would have questioned our parents about the house at one time or another. But we didn't, and our parents never mentioned it or offered explanations as we peered out the car windows at it as we passed. It was an anomaly that existed in the middle of our insular community. It wasn't until years later that we learned it was the home of a man who had mental problems. The tiny house and the fence were built by his parents who lived next door to provide him a place to exist without fear of his wandering off. They had built him a world within a world. Maybe they also built it to protect him from us. Perhaps he was too fragile to interact with the world around him. Whatever the case, we never saw him. If he left the house and wandered inside the fence, it never happened when we were passing by. We had our own Boo Radley living only a couple of miles from our house and never knew it.

Looking back, this was our first encounter with the demons of crazy or knowing of someone who had succumbed to them. I believe that we all have them to some degree. They evolve from insecurities or fears or obsessions or intense desires and grow so quickly and quietly that before we know it they exist within us like impish children playing a game of hide and seek. When we feel strong and brave and want to confront them, they often hide away in some recess or dark corner where we can't find them. And at other times, when we let our guards down or become complacent or are thinking of a million other things, they rear their impish heads sporting sardonic smiles and announce their presence once again. The gentleman that lived in that idyllic house behind that tall fence had apparently lost his battle with them. They sat with him through the long days. They went to bed with him each night.

After we moved from Lick Skillet to our first house in Toney, my brothers and I crossed paths with another person whose demons of crazy seemed to have gotten the upper hand. He was younger, only a couple of years older than my oldest brother. He was tall and thin and had jet black hair. Unlike the man we never really saw, he was out and about on a daily basis. And as I remember, he was always on his bicycle. It's strange that I don't ever remember seeing him off his bicycle, although I know he had to stop from time to time. It is even stranger now that when I ask my aging mother about him, she has no recollection of him at all. It is as if her generation both knew and chose to ignore the people who came from the fringe, or were selective about who they acknowledged in order to keep their peaceful world intact.

I don't recall any interactions with him. I'm sure we must have waved at him from time to time as kids do. But, if he saw us he never acknowledged it. He never stopped. He didn't even look our way as if he were too intent on his destination to even entertain the possibility of a simple glance. I do wonder what he thought about as he rode those countless miles each day. Maybe he never really saw us. Just as the gentleman in Lick Skillet was confined to his little house inside the tall fence, he seemed to be confined to his bicycle. He was afforded more freedom since his demons were apparently not angry ones, or at the least not as controlling. They must have been more like cherubs that kept him company on his rides. If we had been more mature or focused, or had known at the time what to look for, we might have seen them riding on the handlebars of his bicycle or straddling the seat behind him with arms clutched around his waist as they whispered directions in his ear. But, we missed all of that. And still, unlike our parents, we at least always knew he was there.

There were also those, even within our own family, who had succumbed to the demons. All these years later, I am still hesitant to write of them. I can, even now, hear my grandmother's admonitions about not telling all your business. In a hickory nutshell, this meant not to divulge anything about the family that was less than stellar information. She was not in agreement with the southern sentiment that crazy relatives were to be celebrated, embraced and displayed on the front porches. You didn't have to disavow that they existed as long as you were talking to another family member. And even then you were walking on the thinnest of ice. After all, there were always moles trying to obtain any dirt on the Henson family, or so my grandmother thought.

The most prevalent case within our family was an aunt that I never really knew. At a much later time, there was scattered and muted speculation (due to the residual influence of my grandmother) within the family as to the cause of her demons and their eventual success in taking control of her. Of course, speculation is always questionable as it allows us to create sometimes preposterous ruses to explain the simplest of things. In my aunt's case, there was nothing simple about it. It appears to have been as complex as the weaving of vines around the trunk of a tree. It is almost impossible to disconnect one thing from another and regardless of what one believes, in the end my aunt was still the loser.

She lived in a small white house with my uncle, my mother's older brother. The house itself appeared to have arisen from the neighboring swamp. I say arisen because, as in all childhood memories, there are places or buildings that in our minds we don't think existed until we first saw them. That is the way I viewed the house by the swamp. To me it seemed as if the swamp water had defied gravity, flowed upward into the trees and surrounding shrubs and then solidified into the shape of a house. I always wondered how long it would be until the swamp reclaimed it. It is gone now. If there were not a trail of ruts leading off the main road to the place it once sat, it would be as if it never existed at all.

The swamp was the perfect place to grow, nurture and harbor demons. It is no wonder to me that my aunt would have battled them living at its edge. I remember it as a frightful place. Even in the daytime when we walked down the main road that bisected it, we were prone to occasional shivers or chills as if something or someone was walking across our graves (an image given to us by our grandmother, perpetuated by our parents and designed to add to our future neuroses). In addition, there was always the feeling that you were being watched, and that was in the daytime for heaven's sake. At night it was a place to only traverse in the confines of a vehicle, all doors locked and eyes straight ahead. The only time we moved on foot there at night was the result of a sadistic dare and even then you really didn't experience it. You were running so fast that all was a blur including your small heart which seemed to be running ahead of you by at least two yards.

So, it is a natural conclusion that living beside the swamp would have pushed my aunt to be unbalanced and highly susceptible to her demons. Each morning when she stepped out on the porch she would have inhaled the swamp's thick fetid air. At night she would have been bombarded by the sounds of animals and things living there that seemed to come alive in the darkness. There would have been no in-between time for her unless she were away from it. I understand that happened infrequently, and even then I'm not sure she was completely away. She must have carried it with her in her lungs, her mind and even as a distinctive odor in her clothes. In addition, there would have always been the knowledge in the back of her mind that she was going back.

Though I think the swamp alone would have been enough to eventually fracture my aunt's faculties, she was also blessed or cursed, depending on who's telling the story, by an often malevolent husband, my uncle, and an interfering and zealously watchful mother-in-law, my grandmother. If I were describing my uncle in kid's language, I would use the game Red Rover as an analogy. He was the kid, who

27

after calling for you to come over, would wink at you, present a weak linking-of-hands with his teammate, and then as you ran toward him at full speed, would switch to a double-fisted grip. After you picked yourself up off the ground and were able to breathe again, he was the first to hammer you on the back and welcome you to his team. He was that way with my aunt on a daily basis. I don't know if he ever knocked her down, although I do know he encouraged her to fire a shotgun with the butt of the stock held close to her face. Anyone who has ever fired a shotgun can imagine the result. He was both a charmer and an ogre. For my aunt, I guess she never knew which one was calling, "Red rover, red rover."

As far as my grandmother was concerned, she was following the almost typical southern mama mentality in thinking there was really no woman good enough for her sons. When her oldest son married a night club singer, she probably put the hissy into the fits she must have thrown. But fortunately for him and his bride, they moved far away to the north and out of her rays of ill will. For the younger son and his wife, this wasn't the case, as the house by the swamp was nestled at the bottom of a hill where upon sat my grandmother's house, like a watchtower. From her front porch she could monitor the comings and goings as well as the simplest day-to-day tasks of my aunt. She could and did shoot laserlike beams of disapproval or ill will from her eyes. She was like the eye of Mordor in the Lord of the Rings. If there was movement, her eyes would pivot in that direction and lock on to it. She was a giant magnifying glass focusing all her energy on my aunt until tiny wisps of smoke rose off her and spiraled up the hill and filtered into my grandmother's nose.

After the birth of my cousin, her only child, my aunt lasted for several years before she capitulated. It was as if one day with a small suitcase in hand she opened the front door of that small house next to the swamp, stepped out, locked arms with her demons and skipped away. Had I been she, I probably would have dropped the suitcase and flat-out run. Though modern psychology and medicine might have diagnosed her with severe depression complicated by abuse and living in isolation, I still prefer to think it was the demons. If we believe there are demons, we can also believe there are angels. Maybe in her case, it was the demons that became her friends in that lonely place when she needed them most, and then it was the angels that carried her away. From what I know, she did live in an institution for awhile, and eventually recovered. Though she wrote letters to her daughter, my cousin, my grandmother intercepted them. It was years later that my cousin found them and knew that her mother thought of her often. Even with her demons under control, my aunt never returned to the small house by the swamp.

As a grownup I am no longer afraid of the swamp. I have grown to appreciate the beauty of it. I am not fond of the snakes there and am extremely wary when I'm walking close to its brackish water. I have wandered through the weeds and underbrush where the small white house once sat. I didn't hear any whispering or echoes, nor see faint darting figures entering and exiting the nearby brackish water. I have sat on my grandmother's porch at the top of the hill and looked down where my aunt lived and tried to imagine what it would have been like to seek to control and keep track of someone's life. I quickly grew tired of the exercise and could make no sense of what one would gain. Besides, I seem to have enough trouble just keeping up with my own life.

I have driven the road we used to take from Lick Skillet to Huntsville and can find no sign of the tiny house. I guess that is not surprising since the gentleman who lived there must have died long ago along with his family that looked after him. The young man who used to ride the bicycle is another matter however. My middle brother claims to have run into him a couple of years ago in of all places a Publix Supermarket. I wanted to ask if his bike was parked outside, but instead inquired how he knew it was him. He said he looked the same, only older. That was all the information I could get from my brother, as I assume the near encounter rattled him. I know it would have me. I assume his demons were still with him or maybe they too had been replaced by angels like my aunt. They were probably riding in his shopping cart, and though unseen, continuing their job of whispering directions to him. It makes me wonder about the voices I hear inside my own head from time to time. I have always assumed they were my own. Maybe there are times they are not.

The Woods, the Oak and the Great Sadness

The woods and books had always been his salvation. In books he could lose himself, find adventures, become someone else, fill spaces in his head with vivid sweeping images and words that seemed magical on their own. He would carry these stories and words with him to the woods on days when he was filled with such immense joy and happiness that he had to let it spill out before he burst. The woods were also there when a sadness would roll in and overwhelm him to the point he didn't think he could breathe. In the woods it would be tempered. It was as if the trees reached out their limbs and bore part of the weight of it, until he could catch his breath again.

He grew up with two brothers, but they were both much older than he was and they were usually occupied with things that didn't suit him. There were his cousins up the road, but even they would often have different ideas of how the days should be spent. Since he lived so far out in the country, there weren't other kids his age available. Thus, there were many days when he was left to amuse himself. It was on those days that he either lost himself in a book, trilling favorite words off his tongue, or chose to go to the woods and dissolve into the camaraderie of trees. One might think it was his imagination that led to his many beliefs about the trees in the woods, since he had it in abundance due to the large amount of time he spent by himself. In addition, there were the book worlds where he found everything to be possible. But for him, it was all real and a revelation. The woods like his books were a place he belonged without judgment. The trees embraced him like a sapling. While he was there, he was one of their own.

The sounds in the woods were different from what he had become accustomed to. His mother's large family was by nature loud and boisterous. When they were gathered, their voices were always involved in multiple discordant conversations. They constantly talked over each other and subsequently their voices rose like they were climbing the rungs of a ladder. As he and his cousins played outside, there were occasional shrieks, whoops and cries of triumph or disdain, but nowhere near the volume of the adults.

Yet, there were other times when they were mindfully silent. These were the times he relished when they could hear the birds and bugs, the fluttering of trees if there was a breeze, and the occasional conversations of dogs that lived at sometimes great distances from each other. There was rarely the sound of a car on the outlying roads. If they heard one, the sound of its engine seemed to disappear as quickly as it came. They paid the sound little heed as rarely would one move in their direction. On the other hand, the sound of a plane, usually a crop-duster, was such a rarity that it caused them all to cease any activity and gape at the sky for long after it passed. He would think of the word *soaring* and smile as he remembered flying in a book he had read.

When he was in the woods, it was as if even the normal and quieter sounds were muted. The minute he stepped into the edge of the trees it became so quiet that as his grandmother would have put it, "You can hear yourself think." In his head were the words *solitude* and *haven*. As he adjusted to the new level of quiet, he began to hear the trees talk. At first, he didn't know if he were rethinking a story. Words like *impressionable* and *fanciful* popped into his head. Whatever the reason or blessing or even a twist in his own story, he could hear them. They didn't use words, of course. But if he lay against the trunk of the oak tree, he sensed it was reminiscing with the neighboring elm about how they had foolishly competed for the sunlight and sky when they were saplings. Then in a small gust of air that blew over him, he would detect a sigh from the elm as if it too was focusing on their early days so many years ago. Some of their conversations he picked up through touching their trunks like the silver maple's laments about its children caught up in a wind and blown far away. The shag-bark hickory would respond with tales of its offspring being carried off by squirrels or birds. He felt for the first time he understood what the words *languishing* and *forlorn* really meant.

But for the most part, their voices resonated in his head when he climbed them. At one time or another, he scaled them all, including the cottonwoods and pines. If their bottom limbs were too high for him to reach, he would shinny up their trunks until he could catch hold of one. Then he'd pull himself up, throw a leg over and sit until he could catch his breath. From there, he would weave through all their stoutest limbs until he was at a point at the top just before the limbs were too small and new to support his weight. From the top of each there seemed to be a different view even though he was surveying the same woods below. It was as if each tree offered a different scene, as if the view they offered was influenced by their unique personalities. *Perspective* popped into his head. He liked the sound of it and the way it felt when he said it aloud, so he repeated it several times to the trees around him.

He found the pines to have acerbic wits, as they seemed to snicker and chide him on each stain their resin left on his clothes. "A stain no detergent can touch" would play in his head as he shinnied down their trunks to the ground. The cottonwoods would rattle their empty husks, once the seeds were gone, as if to show off their gift for rhythm while he climbed through their branches. His new favorite word *cachucha* both danced in his head and on his tongue. The cottonwoods had the perfect castanets for the folk dance he had read about. On the other hand, the oaks, the maples and the elms never chided nor seemed to feel the need to boast. They were content with their massive limbs and beautiful leaves. If that were not enough, they knew they grew taller than the others. Perhaps the extra sun and their expanded view of the blue sky added to their security. *Panoramic* maybe, he thought. Perhaps, they knew that when he climbed them he could reach higher heights than with the others. Regardless, they all became his friends, even the slightly acerbic pines. Was this what it truly meant to be *tolerant*, he wondered?

The trees perched on the edge of that hillside came to know him so well that they could tell his mood long before he arrived. He would guess their roots were the first to notice a difference in the way he walked across the field to reach them. When he was happy or filled with joy and the desire for adventure, he almost ran to get there. If he was downcast or sad, his feet seemed to become heavier and he often dragged them as he went, tripping over rocks and sticks along the way. However they knew, they seemed to adjust for his mood. On good days, their leaves rustled more and they were more talkative. On sad days, they responded to him only when prompted and seemed more solemn and stately as if they too shared in what sorrow he brought. The meanings of the words *empathetic* and *compassionate* became clearer to him. It was only on the days of great sadness that they seemed lost or perplexed.

He was nine or ten when he first felt the weight of the great sadness. He never knew where it came from or why. He had never read anything to come close to it in his many books. One day he was happy and for the most part content, and then suddenly it was as if a dark cloud descended to surround him and fill his lungs to the point that even breathing became difficult. He didn't cry when it came. It was as if any tears that were in him had dried up and in their place there was only the sadness. There didn't seem to be anything he could do to shake it. Joking brothers, funny shows on TV and even rereading his favorite books couldn't touch it. Fortunately, it usually didn't last long and then it was gone as quickly as it came. But while he was in the midst of it, it took every bit of energy he could muster to hide it. He knew the words *hopelessness* and *despair* from characters that had lost their ways in some of his books. He had felt bad for them and always waited for them to rally. But now, the words not only belonged to him, but had become him. The easiest and seemingly only path for him was to take it to the woods and stay until the worst of it passed. It was on one such day that the great oak saved his life.

His grandmother would have called it the mulligrubs. His mother would have said he was either sulking or in one of his moods. It was enough for him to know that it was neither. He was too young to really understand it to the extent he could explain it. He only knew that it was a great sadness and he carried it with him to the woods. When it had him, the things he normally saw became peripheral. The walk across the field, though a good twenty to thirty minutes in duration, seemed a brief blur. He was so turned in on himself, that all the things he would usually stop to see and marvel at, like a flock of birds that had landed on one of the terraces, a mother with her baby rabbit sitting statuesque with heads turned and ears raised, or even unusual rocks that would have ended up in his pocket, seemed to become insignificant parts of a landscape where he didn't belong. Had he been able to think at all, the word *oblivious* would have shown like a giant marquee in his brain.

At the edge of the woods, he paused. There was a part of him, buried deep within the sadness, that knew he should stop, that it wasn't a good choice. But he felt defeated and hopeless and without any other recourse, so he continued into the woods. As he shuffled through the straw that carpeted the ground, the pines offered no quips. The maples and hickory trees didn't speak of their children. Though there was a slight breeze blowing that day, it seemed all the trees had limited the movement of their limbs and leaves. It was as if they were holding their breaths. *Inevitable* and *preordained* fought to be heard without any remote chance of success.

When he reached the oak tree, the tallest tree in that part of the woods, he immediately began to climb. He didn't stop until he reached the highest point that he had gone to so many times before. The wind had picked up until the gentle breezes became gusts that caused the tops of the trees to dip and sway and draw circles in the sky. He was in no danger as he was ensconced in a solid and safe place in the oak where he had ridden the wind before like a kite or a balloon whose tethering string had been broken. But this time, that was not his purpose. He climbed higher into the younger limbs that weren't yet sturdy enough to hold him. As the dips and sways became more pronounced, he looked down to the ground far below him and wondered how it would feel if he let go and fell. The words *plummet* and *demise* had long belonged to him, but were beyond him in that instant. Would it be painful? Would the sadness be gone for good? Just as in his favorite parts of books when a character seems destined to be lost and is somehow saved in the most inexplicable ways, he felt the young branch he was holding seemingly become larger in his hand. It was as if it was growing too large for him to let it go. At that pivotal moment, the oak whispered in his head, "This is not the time. This is not the way. It will get better, my young friend."

With those words, he felt a lessening of the sadness. It was not gone, but seemed more bearable. He climbed down more carefully than he had climbed up. As he descended, the oak's limbs became larger and more solid. There were moments when his hands touching its weathered bark sensed that it too had known sadness, sometimes from the loss of its favorite saplings or in missing old friends that had succumbed to a long drought. He could hear the words *commiserate* and *sympathetic* somewhere in the back of his head. When he reached the ground, he lay down with his head leaning against the oak. It was close to the spot he would have landed, had he fallen. He lay there long enough for the oak to absorb enough of the sadness within him that he could begin to see the sunlight playing with the leaves on the limbs above him and the swaths of blue sky that changed in shape and size with each gust of wind. He also began to hear a faint murmuring from the other trees. There were no words, only sighs. Though maybe it was the other trees that truly controlled them, the usually acerbic pines held back their jibes. He thought of the word *cathartic* and wondered if it meant when sadness and joy collide with the joy winning in the end. He also wondered if God was in the trees or the trees were part of God. In that moment he better understood the words *reverence* and *blessing.*

The great sadness continued to overtake him at times throughout his childhood. But after that day, it seemed to be more bearable and he learned how to cope with it better. He continued taking it with him to the woods where his friends the trees lived. Each time they would take enough of it away to allow him to breathe more easily, become more hopeful and once again appreciate all the good things around him. The older he got, the less he heard the trees speak. He didn't think they ceased their conversations, but his ability to listen grew less. Still he knew they were always there when he needed them, the pines, the elms, the maples, the hickory trees and especially the tall and majestic oak that saved his life.

Even now, there are days that a doorbell rings in his head and when he answers it the great sadness is there to greet him. It is impossible not to let it in. It is pushy and brash and will not take "no" for an answer. However, he now knows that as a result of it, he has found and experienced his greatest joys. From it comes the words and stories that fill his head. The words dip and sway as if they are perched in the tops of the trees in the gusts of wind, and if he's truly blessed on a particular day, they take flight like phoenixes rising from the ashes. He has also reconnected with words that have gained in significance and have become an almost daily mantra, *perseverance* and *resilience*. Along with his words, books and stories, he still has the woods. It continues to be his salvation. If he is alone there and still for long enough, he can hear the trees whispering. On windy days the whispering becomes words that are almost discernible. At rare times, there is a sound made when a gust of wind causes two limbs to rub against each other. It is a deep and resonant sound like the lower notes on a violin or an oboe. It seems mournful and inviting at the same time. It reaches deep inside him and touches where he knows his soul must be. What he hears are words, "All is good, all is good."

The Dare

My cousin Twalla and I were born four months apart. Since I was born in August and she in the following December, I was eligible to start school before she was. So, for nine months she got to see me ride away on the big yellow school bus each day, while she remained behind with our grandmother. She didn't realize at the time how lucky she was. We were raised more like a brother and sister than cousins. This was primarily due to the fact that my brothers were four and five years older and no other kids lived remotely near. Still, our temperaments matched and we were both adventurous. For the majority of the time growing up, or at least until we were out of high school, we lived either a short distance down the road or across a field from each other. Our mothers were the two youngest sisters of their family and our fathers were friends long before they married the Henson girls.

The two of us were like free range chickens without the feathers, but with all the other scrawny features. Our hair even tended to match, both in color and length, since hers was always cut in a short pixie style. We had about one hundred and forty acres of land that belonged to our grandmother and our parents at our disposal. In addition, there was at least that much if not more across the road where no one had fenced or built houses. We had open fields, woods, creeks, gullies and large trees that were either easy to climb or accessible by steps that someone had added for us. We also had a treehouse my dad had built and vivid imaginations that could make all of this into whatever we wished. We could travel the world and still be home for supper. Weather was never a deterrent. If there was no lightning, the pouring rain would provide another backdrop in our story of the day. Rain-filled ditches were moats to breach on our bikes or on foot to reach the kingdoms beyond. Days of snow provided so many new worlds and possibilities that they were almost too delectable to bear, like the intense sweetness of red velvet cake. If that was not enough, we had what seemed like life-long-days to explore it all.

It was our adventurous spirits that left us open to dares. There were many of them. They came from my brothers, from cousins when they visited and occasionally an uncle who always seemed to chuckle when he voiced them. Sometimes we issued them to each other and when no one else offered them, we often dared ourselves. They were our own version of the Olympics when we could become medal winners for completing difficult tasks. Most dares were simple, like riding our bikes down a particularly treacherous hill, climbing trees that had no limbs low enough for us to reach or swinging on a grapevine across the creek and back. Others involved things that resided in our adolescent fears, such as getting close to the chicken snake in the loft of the barn, riding our bikes or running in the dark on the road through the swamp at night or crawling through dense underbrush to follow the path of a rabbit or some other woodland creature.

There was one dare I remember clearly, and it came from our uncle who was well aware of what would challenge us most and relished offering it up. The most frightening part of it involved where he lived. His house had been built at the bottom of what seemed to us as kids to be a steep hill. At the top of the hill was our grandmother's house, and a path led down from it to our uncle's place. The path led you past Grandmother's barn and then through thick woods. On the other side of his house was the swamp. Each year the swamp seemed to encroach more and more on the land next to his house. So, when we went there, always in the daytime, you could not only smell the swamp or hear the sounds from the critters in it, but also feel it's presence like an ominous being peering over your shoulder. We were thoroughly familiar with the terrain because the path was one of our favorite bike trails. We could ride down it at breakneck speeds, deftly maneuvering over the natural obstacles in our way and then at the bottom, turn and walk our bikes back up the hill to do it again.

There was also a tree near his house that we loved to play in. It was a massive beech tree with low hanging limbs that made it easy for us to climb. The limbs of the tree seemed to form pockets the higher we went. The pockets were natural seats where we could nestle. In the beech, we could pretend to be a on a spacecraft heading for the stars. Each pocket would become part of the ship: a control room, sleeping quarters, a place that the crew would dine, and at the highest point, an observatory where we plotted the course for the mission.

It was on one of these missions that one of us noticed movement in a large knothole in the tree. As we descended for a closer view, it became apparent that the movement was something wet and scaly. The longer we looked we could see that whatever it was had to be more than one. The movie, "Aliens," had not been made yet. If it had, and we had seen it, we would have both duct taped our chests or jettisoned ourselves into deep space. It wasn't aliens though, fortunately for us or unfortunately, depending on how you choose to look at it. It was really a no-win either way. But the realization that it was snakes in the knothole, not only caused us to feel an incredible urge to pee on ourselves, but also elicited our natural flight instinct as we scurried upward to the highest pocket we could reach. This would have been above the observatory, maybe even outside the ship. Using muffled and I'm sure quite shaky voices (as if the snakes could hear us and pinpoint our location) we discussed our options. Since the knothole was located in an area we would have to climb past to get out of the tree, we both knew that escape was out of the question. Our only other choice would be to scream for our uncle and hope the snakes wouldn't hone in on us like rats for supper.

We chose to scream in unison, and our uncle came running out of his front door. When we told him we thought there were snakes in the knothole of the tree, we weren't sure he would help. You see he was quite fond of snakes and very protective of the ones that lived in his garden. But I guess he was more fond of us than the snakes, as he went in his house and got his rifle. After he told us to stay at the highest point we could reach (like we could climb any higher, "Hello"), he began firing shots into the knothole. Snake after snake fell out of the knothole and to the ground below. I don't remember how many there were, just that there were a lot of them. He described their number as a bed of snakes, a strange and shudder-provoking term to describe a gathering of snakes, my cousin and I thought when we were finally given the all-clear sign to climb down out of the tree. We never played in that tree again. But the knowledge of that day in the tree filled with snakes added to the seriousness of our uncle's first dare.

I don't remember why Twalla and I were at our uncle's house that night when the dare was proffered. It must have been the result of running an errand for our grandmother or maybe even a dare from one of my brothers. There must have been a bright moon in the sky or we wouldn't even have considered walking down the path past the barn whose bays looked like gaping mouths in the dark, through the patch of thick woods where only slivers of moonlight could penetrate and then past the huge snake tree, as we now called it. But we were there and had completed whatever mission we were on and ready to make a quick exit when our uncle proffered his dare.

It was a simple one. Yeah, right. Instead of walking back up the path, we had to take the long way back. The long way wasn't really that much farther to go. It was where it took us that made it more frightening. It began with a driveway that was really nothing more than two ruts with a grassy, weedy median that was kept under control by the undercarriages of the cars that rolled over it. The mature trees whose limbs formed a canopy over the road and the underbrush on either side were so thick it was like walking through a tunnel, a tunnel without light. Where the driveway intersected the main road was at the bottom of the hill and at the western border of the swamp. Only deep ditches kept the swamp at bay and after heavy rains even they were not enough. The swamp would rise and cover the road so that cars had to slow to a snail's pace to safely navigate through.

We should have trusted our gut instincts which were obviously in sync as we both had the same terror-stricken looks on our faces. We should have turned around and gone back the same way we came. But you must understand some things about our family. Turning down a dare was the equivalent of becoming a leper. No, you weren't sent away to some godforsaken island to live in a cave for the rest of your life. It was much worse than that. It was as if a scarlet "D" with a slash through it was emblazoned on your forehead. At every family gathering for the rest of your natural life it would be interjected into every conversation. "It's a shame the family lost the farm. If only Twalla and Timmy had taken that dare." "Of course the price of corn is down. The minute they turned down that dare, it was inevitable." Perhaps the worst one that was offered when everyone, but one uncle, was too busy chewing on their chosen pieces of fried chicken to engage in conversation was, "I always thought you kids were Hensons. I guess not, and Opal this noodle dish is truly daring, too daring for some of us."

So, there we were at the end of our very short lives, at the intersection of no turning back and nothing good ahead. Our speed traversing the driveway that night can only be described as almost steady. We didn't want to go too slow for fear of leaving ourselves open to things that might attack us. We didn't want to go too fast for fear of falling and landing on something that moved. We each walked in one of the ruts to avoid the grassy and weedy median where we figured the snakes that didn't live in the tree would surely lurk. The distance between the ruts and the short length of our arms prevented us from holding hands. Even if we could have, it was so dark we wouldn't know for sure whose hand we were holding. That gives me goosebumps just to think about it. Though you would think that talking in low voices might have offered us some comfort, we didn't speak. We were too frightened to utter the simplest of sounds. It was that old "if they can't hear you, they can't find you" theory. In fact, our brains were probably oxygen-deprived as our breathing was labored, if we breathed at all. In kid's time, it took us days to make it to the main road. Once there, we took our first deep breaths. We were halfway through the dare and so far unscathed. All that was left was climbing the steep hill and we'd be safely at Grandmother's house.

In a way the road up the hill was even more frightening than the driveway. It was closer to the swamp, and the smells and sounds seemed to have increased tenfold. Since the trees were not as close to the road, the moon played games with us by spotlighting some areas while leaving others in darkness. Within the spotlighted areas were the ever-changing shadows and shapes created by the limbs of the trees, the bushes that thrived in a swampy terrain, the moss that hung from the trees and birds that prey at night darting across the sky. Our imaginations, that had fed and sustained us on all of those long leisurely days, had now become our worst enemies. No sooner than we could wrap our heads around what each shape or shadow really was, it would change and seem to become something totally differ-ent. We didn't wait long enough to identify them all. We moved at a quicker pace as the solid road beneath our feet meant it was less likely we would step on something ominous or dangerous.

We were almost there when it happened. We had just reached the point where we could see the porch light at our grandmother's house. It was like a scene in a slasher movie when you are yelling at one of the characters on the TV screen, "I know you stabbed him twenty times, cut off one of his hands and shot him in the head, but he's not dead. He's right behind you! Can't you hear the crazy music?" You cover your face because you know the slasher will annihilate them. But since we didn't hear the crazy music, there came a moment of false relief for Twalla and me. We were just a few steps away from safety. If we had been characters in the slasher movie, we would have lit our cigarettes and allowed the smoke to exit our lungs in long languid spirals. We would have high-fived each other and chuckled about how frightened we had been. But like the doomed characters in the movies, we had assumed that the mere suggestion of safety was enough. It was not.

Cue the music from "Jaws." Allow the discordant notes from "Psycho" to intrude on that summer night. It would not have mattered. We would have heard neither. At that moment a dark shape began to rise out of the ditch to our right. It became larger and larger until it towered well above us. It emitted sounds that were almost human, but garbled like they came from a mouth with rows and rows of teeth impeding their clarity. Only one word was emitted from either Twalla or me or maybe from the both of us, "Run!" And we did, perhaps faster than either of us had ever gone, faster than we had ridden our bikes down the hill and faster than Superman had he lived in the swamp. We outran our hearts that throbbed so loudly they could have been the bass in a heavy metal band. We didn't stop running until we had reached our grandmother's porch, launched ourselves through her front door, and then leaned against the door we had locked behind us.

I don't know how long it took our grandmother to calm us down enough for her to understand what we were trying to tell her. Our parents and uncle appeared in what seemed like an instant. That is highly improbable though, since she would have had to call them and at the time we were all on an eight party line. That meant that there were four lines not assigned to family members. If one of the other families was on at the time, I'm sure she would have told them it was an emergency, that something from the swamp had attacked her grandkids and they would have relinquished the line while shuddering from the mere thought of it.

However it transpired, the adults had assembled and our fathers and uncle were on their way down the road to investigate. When they came back, they were laughing. Not even our mothers' or grandmother's laser looks seemed to impede their mirth. It seems that the shadowy figure that rose from the ditch was one of our neighbors who lived about two miles away. He had long ago "lost control of the bottle," as my dad would have put it, like he was driving a car and simply skidded off the road. Anyway, he was highly inebriated and probably on his way to our uncle's house when he staggered and fell into the ditch. When he heard Twalla and me going by, he had risen up to talk to us. Our uncle, who was no longer with our dads, had taken him home.

Had we not been still visibly shaken by the encounter and our shadowy neighbor been present, they would most likely have had us apologize to him for being so rude. It was the way we were raised. Regardless of the situation, we were to be respectful to our elders. Heck, it's a miracle they didn't drive us to his house, so we could say we were sorry for startling him. As our parents shuffled us out the door to our homes, we could hear our grandmother who would always be our defender repeating over and over, "He could have given these kids heart attacks."

I don't know if kids can really have heart attacks, but if they can, Twalla and I were at least close to some coronary damage. Had we been cats, we would have lost one, maybe two, of our lives. Had we been caterpillars, when we became butterflies or really in the case of Hensons, moths, one of our wings would have been damaged or the markings permanently altered. As it turned out, we didn't speak of that night and what happened for a long time. Though members of the family would recount it and laugh, as soon as they saw us close by, their voices would become muffled and all merriment ceased. That included everyone except the issuer of the dare. Our uncle would readily repeat the story in our presence, and while winking, ask us if we were ready for another dare

Now, fifty some odd years later, while Twalla and I are sipping our coffee and catching up on who has passed or hanging on or divorced or remarried or whose kids are where or doing what, we can speak of that infamous dare and the events that ensued that night. We can laugh hardily as we recount it all, but inevitably one or sometimes both us will shudder. We've neither said it, but probably both of us have thought that living on that deserted island wouldn't have been such a bad thing. In addition, if being a Henson means risking your life on a dare, then maybe a name change would be better. "A Henson by any other name would smell as sweet." I don't know if "sweet" is even plausible where our family is concerned. But one thing is for sure, we would at least still have one of the lives we lost that night.

Things My Dad Built

My dad was extremely good looking and muscular. He also suffered from what we now know to be manic depression. The first two things were evident, but the last one we never knew until he got much older. Looking back now, I think he dealt with his depression by always staying busy. Maybe he was given this treatment option from his father who was certainly responsible for most if not all of his depression, either genetically or by not providing the affirmations my dad needed while he was growing up. I think the latter is probably most to blame, because my dad went overboard trying to affirm everything my brothers and I did. Too much affirmation can be just as detrimental as too little, as in the way my dad overcompensated with my brothers and me. He made us believe we were the cat's meow, when in truth we were more like the gigantic fur ball the cat hacked up. Unfortunately for me, I didn't inherit his looks or musculature. I was blessed with the genetic code from my mother's side of the family, skinny legs with knobby knees, a bulbous nose, bad teeth, a spastic colon and hair that jumped off my head before I turned twenty years old. I did inherit some of the depression bit from my dad, but not the building bug to cope with it.

Anyway, following the proverb, "the idle mind is the devil's workshop," my dad stayed busy. He even took the workshop bit to heart. He became a self-taught carpenter. "Self-taught" is key here since he truly had no inherent building skills. He didn't work from blueprints. He just built things. Some things turned out to be functional. Some did not. All were flawed in various ways. But no one ever pointed them out, except for my mother. She viewed everything with a critical eye. She may have been another reason that my dad stayed busy building all the time.

His earliest constructions were sheds or outbuildings as they were called at the time. Wherever we lived he constructed one or sometimes two. This was practical, since at the time there weren't prefab buildings to purchase. So if you needed a place to store outdoor tools and machines, you had to build it. It is true that the more he built, the better they looked in design. But the first ones, though functional, were not attractive. They would have fit right in on the plains of the Midwest during the depression. He would start okay with a basic square or rectangular building. But then, as if possessed by the spirit of a deranged carpenter, he would add on parking bays or even rooms. In the end, the building looked like a courthouse in a shanty town.

I shouldn't be offering so many negatives here. As a kid growing up in the country with an absolutely mandatory imagination, the early buildings were a godsend. The nooks and crannies became escape routes for me at ten years old when I had been unjustly imprisoned, of course. They were the headquarters for international spy rings. I escaped going to church at times by hiding in them. Sometimes, they became my church where I could have seriously needed conversations with someone who would understand my warped point of view. I spent hours alone in the various additions my dad added. So, in a way, his crazy world also became mine.

Buildings were not the only results of his questionable carpentry skills. He also built pieces of furniture for my mother. I will give my mother credit here. I'm sure she wasn't totally pleased with what he built her. But then again, she also knew there wasn't sufficient money to purchase the items from a store. She probably did a lot of lip biting, which of course led to my later proclivity for fever blisters (stretch, I know, but trying not to blame everything on genetics). Also, my mother was very practical. She made all her clothes. They were actually all cut from the same pattern, just different fabrics to throw off the most discerning eyes.

Anyway, the piece of furniture I remember most, and that appears in the background of numerous pictures my father took, was a display cabinet. It was pretty well constructed, but strangely non-functional. Its purpose was to house my mother's collection of salt and pepper shakers that were all figurines representing various countries from around the world. She picked them up on each trip that we took. Oddly enough, we never left the United States. So, our travels were certainly limited. This leads me to a question I have never asked her. Where the heck did she get them all? I mean, do you just walk into a souvenir shop in Brunswick, Georgia and ask if they have any salt and pepper figurines from Sweden? And someone doesn't question your sanity while responding, "why yes we do?" Anyway, the cabinet my dad built was huge. But there were only maybe five small shelves all housed deep inside it. It would only hold about twelve of the countless figurines she had. In addition, if the cabinet were not turned just so toward natural light, the figures looked like they were standing in the back of a grotto like in Rock City.

He also built things for my brothers and me. One winter we had the biggest snow that I can remember. It must have been at least a foot

deep. This is not an exaggeration, since there are of course pictures
of us in drifts with the snow up to our waists. It was perfect for sled-
ding and we had just the right spot, since our grandmother lived up
the road on a big hill. However, no one we knew had a sled. We lived
in Alabama for gosh sake. Who had money to shell out for a sled that
might be used once in a century? So, my father tunneled his way
out to his shanty town workshop and built us one. My brothers and
I were beyond excitement as we dragged the sled the half mile or so
to our grandmother's house. The key word here is dragged. Had I
used the word pulled or guided or even steered, the outcome might
have seemed brighter. But no, we had to drag it. It must have taken
us an hour to traverse the distance to the top of the hill. Once there,
we argued for another half hour as to who would be the first rider. In
the end it was the oldest brother. So, my middle brother and I stood
back and watched as he positioned the sled on the road where the hill
began its steepest descent. He strode back a good ten feet so that when
he ran and boarded the sled he would achieve maximum speed. It is
a miracle that he didn't break a bone, because when he launched into
the air and landed on the sled, it didn't move even an inch forward.
It sank so quickly and so deeply that it had to rattle his teeth. Need-
less to say, my middle brother and I didn't even try it. All I can say
is thank heavens once again for cardboard boxes. We got some from
our grandmother and rode them until they became too soggy to slide.

The sled was not my dad's last attempt at producing something to
keep us occupied while living at the time in what we considered to be
the middle of nowhere. When my cousin and I expressed an interest
in sailing the high seas, that in our case and also location involved the
pond in the middle of the cow pasture, he was quick to action. We had
caught him at the right time. There was really nothing else he could
logistically add to his outbuildings. Our house was full of furniture.
The salt and pepper shakers not housed in the grotto were ensconced
safely in another more functional bookshelf he had built. So, before
anyone could say, "shiver me timbers," he was back in his workshop

constructing a raft. When he finished, we were elated. After all it had all the looks of a fine raft, solid and square and like it might even float, that is to 10-year-old kids. As he helped my cousin and I carry the sleek sailing vessel to the pond, we could already see ourselves as Huck Finn or even Captain Ahab. We were sure we would be able to both carry Big Jim to freedom and also spear the great white whale while on our way.

So, without the usual christening ceremony, my cousin and I boarded our country yacht ready to sail the churning seas. The pond water was churning because the cows had just had their midday baths. Since they didn't adhere to rules about not using the bathroom in the pool, they had also made their customary deposits. When we first set foot on the raft, all seemed fine. It moved slowly away from the bank and we began our leisurely cruise. Then, as if Poseidon himself had reached up from the bottom of the pond and grabbed hold of the raft, one side sank into the water. My cousin and I slid into the water as the raft without our weight resumed its original horizontal position and floated away. You see, my dad had not attached any buoyant devices beneath the raft to account for our weight. He had simply constructed what was essentially a wooden pallet. My cousin and I weren't daunted by the failure of our sailing vessel. We just laughed as we swam about sputtering and gargling in the pond water. We were much like a video game, had there been any at that time, dodging cow patties that floated all around our heads. My dad was laughing on the bank until he heard the shrill voices of my mother and aunt demanding that my cousin and I get out of the pond. It seems they didn't understand the benefits of ingesting water infused with cow urine and feces. I think it made us stronger.

Now, when I watch those commercials with the message that something is "Ford Built," it reminds me of all those things that were "Dad Built." They were never perfect and many times they weren't functional. They were all fed by his need to cope with the depression that he fought daily. If he were alive today, I would offer him the affirmation his dad neglected to provide. I would marvel at all the things he built and tell him how wonderful and beautiful they were. I'd also tell him that I need a duplicate of that first display cabinet he built, so I could have a place to house the salt and pepper shakers I inherited. With the addition of a few LED lights in the dark recesses of the cabinet, it would no longer be a simple display. It would be a tourist attraction that just might give a small unincorporated town a claim to fame. See Rock City? Why bother when there's something just as inspiring in Toney, Alabama?

The Rabbit Hunt

I think there were more snowy days when we were growing up than there are now. In addition, there was rarely a light dusting or shower of snow that melted on the warmer ground. The skies would darken, as the clouds became heavy with the moisture that would freeze in the frigid air and then suddenly what seemed like a kajillion snowflakes would fall. They were so big and fluffy that the things we were used to seeing from the window were obscured. It was as if a white gauzy curtain enveloped our house. When the snowfall subsided, the whole landscape was transformed. Where there were ditches, there now appeared to be level ground. Bushes and shrubs appeared to be small animals guarding the house while the trees became glistening white giants. There would be an incredible silence as the snow seemed to absorb the slightest sounds. There was no way any vehicles could move, even if they could have located the roads. Everything typical was halted which meant for us the blessing of all blessings, no school!

For my older brothers, cousin Twalla and me these heavy snowfalls meant the building of snowmen, the construction of snow forts and numerous snowball fights waged intermittently throughout the daylight hours. If it was also a lucky day, it opened the possibility of a rabbit hunt. Rabbit hunts were always led by our Aunt Dudie, Twalla's mother, my mother's sister and the youngest of seven children in the Henson family. I really don't know where the nickname Dudie came from, but we always guessed she was prone to a certain kind of accident as a child.

I do know where my cousin Twalla's name originated. It seems that while Aunt Dudie was visiting her husband who was in the navy and stationed in California, her mode of transportation had to be the most economical. At that time it meant traveling by bus. For most of the trip she was sitting next to a lady and her young daughter who were of Mexican descent. According to Dudie, the child was not only beautiful, but also had an angelic disposition. The child's name was Twalla Marquita. Thus, my cousin received a unique and exotic name. Unfortunately, it was tacked on to a common, not so unique and even less exotic last name, Smith.

The rabbit hunts never endangered any animals. Peter Rabbit and his crew were not scheduled for execution. We were merely following the tracks the rabbits left in the snow as they went on their merry ways. I use the word "merry" here because when I think of rabbits I see their bushy round tails, their ears stretched high toward the sky, whiskers gyrating at the slightest sound and the soulful look in their large eyes and I think "merry." Come to think of it, it is odd that we never had one as a pet. My brothers and I had dogs, cats, chickens and even a cow. Yes, we had a pet cow. Her name was Blacky. She would come to the fence when my brothers and I were outside. We'd feed her by hand and rub on her head. Then one day when we came home from school she wasn't there. Well, she was there, but in a different form. She was on the supper table that night on our hamburger buns. I don't know if it was me or one of my brothers that put it all together. But, someone muttered the name Blacky. Our parents exchanged a conspiratorial glance as they took huge bites of their burgers. For that one night, my brothers and I were herbivores. The chickens we raised and sometimes carried around in our arms followed that same path to the table. So, I guess it was good we never had a pet rabbit. If we had had one his name would have had to have been Stu.

Another reason the rabbits were safe from us is because we weren't raised to be hunters. There was a rifle and a shotgun in our house, but our dad just didn't have the heart to shoot anything wild. On the other hand, he didn't mind hooking fish. Our mother and dad loved to fish. They could spend what seemed an eternity to my brothers and me, fishing from the bank or a boat. They only paused to eat crackers and Vienna Sausages or potted meat sandwiches. At different times we were all subjected to the fishing marathon. None of us took to it like our parents. There was just too much down time. We needed cliffhanging excitement like walking for miles in the snow-covered woods looking for rabbit tracks. I think Marlin Perkins would have been proud of us, but I don't think we would have ever been featured on *Wild Kingdom*.

There was one particular rabbit hunt where the only thing endangered was me. The day started with a sky so intensely blue that it reflected on the snow. The bluish tint gave the snow an even more ethereal appearance. It was a deep snow that filled all the ditches and gullies as if they had never been there. Tree limbs sagged from the weight of it. Bushes became shapes that suggested an invasion of dwarfish creatures that lay in wait for unsuspecting victims who came their way. It was so cold that a thin layer of ice had settled during the night over the snow making it glisten in the sunlight like it was embedded with tiny diamonds. Coupled with the blue from the sky, it was as if God had made our farm into a rich jewel field where fortunes could be made.

Dressing for the hunt that day posed several problems for my brothers and me. We were not poor in relation to many of the kids we went to school with, but there wasn't an abundance of money either. Certainly there wasn't enough to purchase adequate clothing for winter excursions. We all had boggins. Our grandmother made sure of that every Christmas. We also had gloves, although they weren't the waterproof kind. Maybe those weren't even available then. Even so, ours were the knit kind, usually acquired from an aunt or uncle who had sat in the corner during our Christmas gathering, chuckling when we opened our presents from Grandma, knowing we'd soon open the gloves from them and affording them the opportunity to gleefully espouse, "Oh look, gloves to match your boggins. You lucky kids!" We had coats and sweaters, but we didn't have boots. So, under our mother's supervision, we layered shirts and sweaters and put on at least two pairs of socks. Then, somehow we managed to squeeze into two pairs of pants. At that point, when it was almost impossible to bend, we laced up our Converse All Stars. We were smart enough to know our tennis shoes weren't waterproof. So, our final piece de resistance was to pull a pair of socks over our shoes and shove the bottoms of our pants into them. As ludicrous as it sounds, it was the best we could do. If we fell, we wouldn't be getting up. Heck, we could barely maneuver out the door. Of course, Twalla and Aunt Dudie appeared wearing waterproof boots as well as other appropriate winter attire. I guess that was one of the perks of being in a one-child family.

On this day, what we wore was no match for the bone chilling cold as we set off across the field behind our house toward the woods at the back of the property. We appeared to be a motley crew, indeed, with Dudie and Twalla dressed like they could have been in an ad from a sportsman's catalog and my brothers and me looking like we were transients wearing all the clothing we possessed to avoid carrying a knapsack. We all had to acquire sticks along the way, per Aunt Dudie's instructions, not for the thrashing of rabbits we found, but to poke in the snow ahead of us to ensure that there was solid ground below. She also assured us the sticks would come in handy should we happen on what looked like a rabbit's lair. The sticks could be used to probe into the lair and encourage the rabbit to exit and scurry away. I leave out the word "merry" here, because I don't think the rabbit would be so happy to leave its home so abruptly. She never explained what purpose this served other than, I guess, that we would be able to deem the hunt a huge success in that we had successfully tracked, found, and rousted a rabbit from its peaceful slumber. Of course, we could also exclaim like a children's chorus, "Hey look, a rabbit!"

So, onward we trudged making crunching sounds as our feet broke through the layer of ice that had settled on the snow. For my brothers and me the crunching sound was muffled a bit because of the socks over our shoes. The bitterly cold air made our breaths hold close to our faces and then swirl around our heads forming what looked like cloud covers over our boggins. There were no tracks to be found in the first field we crossed. A late dusting of snow that had fallen during the night along with the morning icing had covered them all. But in the woods, Aunt Dudie told us, the trees would have buffered some of the snowfall and there we would find them. Like true innocents under a spell, we believed every word she said. She wasn't a wicked witch. She was more like Glenda, the good witch of the north, and she was leading us into Munchkinland where rabbit tracks were better than a yellow brick road.

We were already shaking from the cold when we entered the woods. It became worse as we pushed in and around and under huge tree limbs weighted down with snow. Anytime a limb was brushed against what seemed like an avalanche would fall onto anyone near. The snow would somehow find its way down inside our collars. It would blanket our faces. There would be a moment in which you felt smothered by it. At first, we were gleeful at the sight and the feel of it and then the cold and wet would seep in and make us shiver even harder.

Just when we were ready to give up, Aunt Dudie stopped and pointed with her stick to what had to be the tracks of some small animal in the snow. Off we went renewed by the excitement of it and with an altered vision. The snow-covered limbs changed from things that brought pain to things of beauty. We saw the icicles that dangled from the tips of branches. Once again the ground seemed bejeweled. We were aware of the quietness of the place with the snow muffling all sounds, other than our breaths which became slower and more controlled so as not to disturb anything. As we followed the tracks, we became more focused and stealthy like we were members of an NCIS team careful not to disrupt any part of a crime scene.

The tracks ended at the edge of a small creek that had frozen over. I don't know what really possessed me to want to step onto the frozen creek. Even though it looked solid, I knew there was always the possibility that it wasn't strong enough to hold my weight. Not even my middle brother's warning to not even think about it deterred me. In fact, I moved quickly so that no one else could stop me. It was a foolish blunder of vast proportions. As soon as both my feet were on the ice, a cracking sound rose up to find my boggin-covered ears. At that point there was no time for retreat, no back pedaling, no second thoughts and no slow motion Kung Fu flipping maneuver to save me. One second I was on the ice and the next I was in the creek with water cresting just below my knees. The temperature of the water had to be just above freezing. The only reason it had not become more solid was because it was a running creek.

I don't know if the tears started then, or after my brothers helped me out, but they came in torrents and soon I was sobbing. On cold and snowy days sobbing takes on a more visual presence, with breath being drawn from the bottom of your lungs and coming out an almost solid white. I must have resembled a steam engine. My Aunt Dudie put her arms around the heaving shoulders of the little steam engine I had become, the one that all of a sudden knew he couldn't continue the hunt and told me I needed to go home as quickly as I could manage. I didn't wait to hear if there was muffled laughter. There probably wasn't any as they knew how miserable I felt. I don't remember much about the walk back home. I was relieved that no one was with me. The half- to three-quarters of a mile I had to walk was blurred by tears, frustration, and an incredibly aching numbness that took over my feet and legs. When I arrived, my mother made me immediately strip off my wet clothes and put me in a hot bath. It is a miracle that I didn't suffer any physical damage like frostbite.

On those coldest of days when you could see your breath hovering before you, it was almost like there were words hidden there if you looked quickly enough before they could disappear. The blanket of snow that could make the ugliest of things appear pristine and pretty could also hide places of danger. It could all be scraped away with a rabbit hunting stick to uncover what truly lay beneath. Add to it all the surrounding silence interrupted only by the cadence of your own labored breathing, and it would become the perfect scenario to learn about yourself, how pretty things were not always what they seemed and that dangerous things were often hidden. Other than the knowledge that we were incredibly blessed to be with our aunt on adventures into the snowy woods, we all learned something. I don't know what my brothers or cousin learned on those hunts. As for me, I learned that there was always a delicate balance of sadness and joy inside of me. In the woods on those cold winter days, I often found both. But most importantly, I discovered I was resilient. The little steam engine in the story discovered it really could climb the hill. I learned that I could do the same.

The Rain, the Willow and Brothers Three

The three of us are glued to the picture window in the living room watching the rain coming down in torrents. We are quiet and listening for the sound of thunder. Our eyes are glancing right and left for flashes of lightning in the clouds. It seems forever before my oldest brother pensively calls to our mother in the kitchen, "There's no lightning or thunder. Can we go out?"

Our mother with a dishcloth in her hands walks to the window and looks out to evaluate the storm. Without turning to look at us, she seems to offer to the rain outside as much as us, "Put on your old tennis shoes. At the first sound of thunder, I want you back in the house."

We barely hear the last of her words as we race to put on our shoes and then fly out the back storm door. Within seconds we are drenched and laughing. The rain runs off the tops of our heads and drips into our eyes and mouths. When we turn to look upward, it is like looking through a windshield with the light of the daytime sky muted by the curtain of water covering it. We are water creatures moving like statues in three separate fountains across the yard.

The large drainage ditch to the east of the house is our first destination. We charge into it with reckless zeal, feeling the current trying to pull our feet out from under us. We stomp and march against the fast flowing water as the rain saturates the surrounding fields causing the runoff to continually replenish the already-engorged ditch. We find sticks to float in it and we walk along the sides to track their progress. Many of our stick ships are lost in the current or trapped in eddies that form along the way. We try to dislodge them with bigger sticks we find. Even so, some of them are given up as lost. We are not good river traders. Thank goodness no towns or villages are counting on us and the goods our ships provide to survive. It is all too fleeting with us. There is too much else to do. The shipping business is closed until further notice.

On these most magical days when rain falls without the claps of thunder or the flickering of lights from the electricity in the air, there is no down time, not a moment to pause or be still. As soon as the stick ships are abandoned one brother yells, "Get the bikes!" The rain stings our faces as we dash to the shed. We are a wet blur on our bikes as we slide and skid while creating jets of water from our spinning tires. We ride through the water that rises over our pedals. We ride in and out of the ditch as if it is a slalom course and when we reach the road, we ride back to the start and do it all again. We ride until our legs grow tired from fighting to pedal against the resistance of the water. And still the rain falls into our eyes and our mouths when we yell to each other.

From the ditch we head to the terraces in the field behind our house. The rise and fall of the terrain makes for perfect riding on clear days. We have ridden them so much that permanent trails now mark our paths. But, on rainy days even the trails become new and more special. Tiny rivulets of water crisscross the trails. The places where our tires always gripped on dry days suddenly provide no traction. We become a slow motion ballet as we slide around corners or scream until our mouths are full of water and our brakes cease to stop our momentum. Arms flail to adjust and balance. Legs thrust right and left to fulcrum against falls. And all the while our wheels spiral water into the air surrounding us. We could be the country version of *Swan Lake* produced in a water park. We have the ugly duckling part down, but there don't seem to be any swans hatching out from the rain and mud that now covers us from head to toe.

Our final destination is like a rainy day car wash for people on bicycles. It is the huge weeping willow directly behind our house. When we ride through its branches they feel like the rubber swishers of a car wash. They fold onto our bodies seeking to wet any area that has managed to stay dry so far. Then we're in the safe dry space under the tree where you can hear the rain, but no longer feel it. And just as suddenly we reach the other side where the swishers are waiting for us once more. As we grow more tired from the soaking and the exercise, we pause more and more under the willow.

The willow tree is one of my zones. It is where our dad has hung a rope and wood swing for me. It is where I almost daily compete in gymnastic events, performing only the most difficult flips and dismounts. However, it is not a zone for my oldest brother. It is here that he almost lost his face and maybe his life. It started on such an innocent note. We were without a dog and someone had one they needed to give away. It was a male, always a good attribute our parents thought, and his name was JoJo, a seemingly delightful name for a dog from the breed called boxers. He was tied to the trunk of the weeping willow until he could acclimate to his new home and to prevent him from running off until that happened. The detail not shared with our parents was that JoJo had never been around children. We were used to dogs of all kinds by this time. Our parents trusted us to present ourselves to JoJo in a slow, methodical and nonthreatening manner. Perhaps they gave us too much credit for having common sense. We could have told them it was something that all three of us were lacking.

On the first day we got him, we learned JoJo would growl when we got within a few feet of him. Move one foot closer and he would chase you until the rope restraining him pulled taut. "Perfect," we all three thought. We would take turns running into the two foot range, engaging JoJo's disgust that we were so close, then racing to the other side of the tree with him nipping at our heels until his rope restrained him. What a mirthful game we had constructed. All was going great until two factors came into play. First, JoJo didn't really consider it a game. He didn't know us well enough to engage in play. And second, our lack of common sense didn't help us in assessing the danger of the situation. We had not allowed for the possibility of tripping or falling and there was no plan B in place in case there was an issue with JoJo's rope. Unfortunately, for our oldest brother, both factors came into play at the same time. As he ran the tried-and-true pattern under the weeping willow, he tripped just as he reached what had been the safe zone on the other side. Even then he would have been okay had JoJo's rope not stretched that extra foot. In a flash our brother was on his back with what was now a very angry boxer straddling his face with a paw on each side of his head. I'm sure the growl our brother heard was much worse than the one we heard from our safe positions. Fortunately for him and unbeknownst to us, our mother, knowing we weren't the sharpest tools in the shed, had been watching. She raced out of the house, grabbed the other end of JoJo's rope, pulling him off my brother who didn't need instructions to skedaddle into the house. Of course, that was JoJo's last day with us.

We weren't allowed to talk to our brother about that event, and as we should have been, we were all chastised for teasing the dog. It is possible he would have eventually been a good dog for us. However, it is also possible that he might have taken one of us down and hidden what was left in the storm drain, like Cujo. We understood the not talking about it, as even on this rainy day while we are riding our bikes in and out of the shelter of the willow, we can tell it is not a shelter for our brother. The rain reminds him of the hideous slobber that dripped on his face, and the willow was almost the last thing he saw.

Our pause under the willow gives us that last burst of energy to ride our bikes back into the rain. This time we are not up for the slaloms or the ditches. It is to the road in front of our house we head. It is easy riding for a spell with our wheels scattering the water on the asphalt. We only have to pedal a little harder to pass our aunt's house on the left and then reach our grandmother's at the top of the hill. We pause there like skiers at the top of jump. It is a much steeper descent on this side. I am hesitant though I would never tell my brothers. I am too happy to be included and fearful that they won't ask me again if I complain. It is stopping that is my concern. On a dry day it is doubtful that my brakes will hold or that I can even control my bike if they do. On this day the roads are wet and I can see ahead that the swamp at the bottom has filled the ditches on either side to overflowing and completely covered the pavement in spots.

But when my oldest brother raises his arm and points forward, I follow them into the plummet. It is a couple of minutes that seem like a whole lifetime to me. We are moving so fast that the rain stings when it hits my face. All else is forgotten. There is no JoJo for my oldest brother. There is no worry about my bicycle's brakes for me. We are a blur of rain and the best of childhood when we hit the area where the water covers the road. The water rises up to meet the rain coming down and we seem to become a wave surging toward the shore. And then it ends as suddenly as it began. Any parts of us that had dried under the willow are now wetter than before. The three of us are laughing and sputtering water. We are shaking from the exhilaration and I am wondering if there ever could be a better feeling. But that feeling passes too quickly because now I remember we have the hill to climb to get back.

Even for my older brothers the steepness of the hill is a challenge. The goal is always to ride all the way to the top without stopping. For me, on this rainiest of days, I am doubtful that I can do it. It requires the strongest of pedaling from a standing position to pull the hill. My brothers take deep breaths and then charge it as they always do. I follow behind and wish with all my might that this will be the time I'm successful. I don't want the camaraderie to end. I want their respect. I want them to see me as an equal. As we hit the hill, the rain seems to increase in volume and is now blowing against us. I am halfway up when I see them at the top waiting for me. I push my legs until they burn. Only ten more feet to go when I feel my bike slowing to the point that the front wheel begins to wobble. This will not be the day. I have to stop and push my bike the final few feet. If they are disappointed in me, they don't show it. They both pat me on my wet back and we ride the rest of the way back to our house.

By the time we arrive, we have that happy tired feeling and are soaked through and through. We put our bikes in the shed and walk to the house where our mother is waiting with a stack of towels in her hands at the door to the utility room. "All the wet clothes and shoes off now and completely dry yourselves. I don't want any water on my floors," she tells us as she smiles and shakes her head.

I don't know what my brothers are thinking as we go our respective ways in the house. For me, it is always a good day when they include me in what they are doing. I have kept up with them for the most part and done everything they did except for the hill. One day I will pull it on my bike without stopping. I only hope that on that day, whether it is raining or not, that one or both of them is there to see it. It will be a passage of sorts and passages should always be shared. It is my brothers I want to share it with. I can hear the rain still drumming on the roof as the warmth of my dry clothes seeps into my skin and I fall asleep on the couch with my head resting on the side of the hill.

The Choosing

L ong before the *Hunger Games*, our family had an equally bizarre ritual where a choosing was involved. It did not lead one to a fight to the death, but rather a fight for breath. We didn't have names like Katniss or Petyr, but we did come from a family with a penchant for unusual monikers. We had an Uncle Slats (substituted for his real name Vermon) and an Uncle Verbon (certainly no coincidence). There were great aunts, Verdie, her sister Merdie and great uncles Ransom and Bamar. There was even a cousin named Whistle-britches until the Army forced him to change it to something more acceptable. Of course our favorite as adults was an older very distant cousin named Anita Dick. Yes, Dick. We were descended from a long line of Dicks. Though as kids, we were not equipped with enough knowledge or social savvy to know we should have been insulted when a distant relative squeezed our cheeks and intoned, "Why you've got Dick written all over you. Come here Bamar and look at this little Dick."

Anyway, the Dick in us did not lead to "The Choosing." What really set the stage for it was our fathers' proclivity to drinking, partying and having a good time. It was actually their pursuit of alcohol-induced revelry that led to the expansion of our family. My father was dating my future mother. His best friend wanted him to go drinking with him in Tennessee. My father countered with the idea that he should meet his girlfriend's sister. They flipped a coin and his best friend lost or won, depending on who is telling the story, like my aunt for instance. So they married sisters and with them came their two brothers, who were also no slouches in the drinking department.

Since there was never a question that these men were going to drink, the wives agreed to have parties, because in their minds their husbands would be under their noses if they became inebriated and subsequently less apt to get into any "meanness," as the family termed it. So parties were planned at various houses, and we were always sent to Grandma's house to spend the night. What we didn't know at the time was that all these factors, including the infamous coin toss, swirled around in the cosmos to a central point of confluence just above her house, creating optimal conditions for "The Choosing."

We loved and adored our grandmother. She spoiled us unmercifully, but there were some things on which her mind was fixed and I can't remember a time when she wavered. First of all, she did not believe in air conditioning. All that was available at the time were window units which any one of her brood would have gladly bought her, except for one uncle, who had his hands full with his second wife who declared that giants were stooping down to look in the windows of their small house. Grandma not only refused them, but would always go into a tirade about how air conditioning was the reason we stayed sick so much. She didn't take into account that we were a sickly lot to begin with and had consumed mass quantities of creek water while swimming.

We probably had more of those microscopic squiggly things living in our guts than in a laboratory petri dish in a third world country. At Grandma's house, which sat on the highest point of a seventy-acre farm, air circulation was achieved through the raising of all windows and opening the front and back doors. If the air didn't come through those screens, then according to Grandma, it wasn't good for you anyway.

Second, Grandma had ideas of bedtime which must have come from the Middle Ages. If you weren't in the house and in bed by dark, you were subject to being bitten by a rat carrying the plague, or worse, hit on the head by someone. This probably led to our first true feelings of ambivalence. We were faced with both that wonderful period of time when we had free reign of the farm to do as we pleased, and when tired to return to the house and be spoiled by as many fried pies as we could consume while listening to our Grandma's sweet voice telling us how wonderful we were. Sitting on the floor around her we looked like a motley and nasty crew of street urchins resting at the feet of a master thief and waiting to be sent out to pick a pocket or two. And of course at the same time, in the backs of our minds was the knowledge that there was a flip side to the visit. There would be the dreaded bedtime and it would come as soon as it got dark outside.

It was the convergence of her two mindsets that truly led to "The Choosing." As the darkness approached, we all became more and more apprehensive. We immediately began to frantically scheme. If someone feigned illness, perhaps, or tearfully presented an injury incurred during one of our games or claimed one of us had been hit on the head, maybe we could alter the course of the evening. What we ended up doing was learn to be deft controllers of the three channels on the black and white TV set in her living room. You see, Grandma absolutely loved three shows and wouldn't miss them. She tapped her toes as Lawrence Welk's orchestra played, occasionally commenting about how cheap one of the singers looked with her hairdo that week, or cooing when the Lennon sisters sang, wistfully thinking that that could be her own daughters singing, even though none seemed to have inherited our grandfather's gift for music. She was also obsessed with a local celebrity named Grady Reeves. We never figured out what she saw in this rather rotund man in glasses, who talked a lot and regularly laughed at his own jokes. But to Grandma, if Grady said it, well, it was like gravy on hot mashed potatoes. Finally, our diminutive and sweet grandmother adored wrestling. There were matches that were broadcast from the local coliseum. There was nothing that could make her more animated than to watch wrestlers with names like Tojo Yamamoto and Jackie Fargo throw each other around the ring. If we were lucky, we could find those three shows on different channels faster than Grandma could utter the word bedtime. If we failed, it would be time for "The Choosing."

I don't think summers then were hotter than they are now. Still, on those summer nights at Grandma's house, especially at bedtime, air seemed to stand still. It was as if it had been tied to the ground. Trees sat motionless. Crickets didn't chirp. The air was too thick for them to move their legs. Frog's didn't eat, since flies couldn't move their wings in the hot sorghum-like air. As kids, we would lie on the floor next to the front screen door and press our faces so hard into the screen that I'm sure Helen Keller could have read the bits of our flesh that pressed through. She would have probably looked both perplexed and a bit shocked by what her fingers read uttering, "Dicks. Got Dick written all over their faces."

The most dreaded time of our young lives had arrived. We willed ourselves smaller, more nondescript, crawled behind chairs, fought with each other for closets, tried to lie motionless and blend into the old rug on the floor, or get as close to her feet as we could hoping she would over-look us. None of our ploys worked. I'm not sure that she really thought much about it. I never saw her with a list she checked off. She never had a bowl like in the *Hunger Games* from which she drew a name. She would just stand up from her chair, say it was time for bed and utter the name of "The Chosen," the unlucky cousin who would sleep with her that night. There should have been more air in the house at that moment, since there were so many huge sighs of relief. But there seemed to be less, as the one who had been chosen sucked up every breath released from the other cousins as if storing up for what was to come.

Now lest you think otherwise, our grandmother was not someone to dread sleeping with. She did have a strange old person smell which I guess I'm developing now that I'm getting to that age range. She was clean and not a clinger. It was just that on top of her bed, year round, was a goose down-filled feather mattress. When you climbed into bed with her you immediately rolled to the middle and wedged against her. I don't think even grappling hooks would have helped you escape. The mattress would encase you and Grandma like two mummies. It felt like you were buried alive. You would have shouted had there been breath to spare, "Hey I'm not dead yet!" It wouldn't have mattered anyway. The other cousins were all plastered on the screen door and the mattress was so thick the words would have been muffled by the feathers. So for what seemed a lifetime, you could not move or breathe. You listened to Grandma snore and watched what little there had been of a childhood pass before your eyes. Near the end of it, before you thought an ending was possible, you would wish for the river Jordan and a sweet chariot coming for to carry you home.

Then out of nowhere came the morning. You looked and Grandma was gone, and if you shifted your weight just a little, the sides of the mattress would start to lie down. You climbed out of the bed like an Eskimo leaving an igloo, like a bug leaving a cocoon. I can't say butterfly, because none of us were to become butterflies, moths maybe, but I'm really thinking mealy bugs, if they were ever in cocoons. You could smell the wonderful breakfast Grandma was cooking, hot biscuits baking and country ham frying and you could hear the laughing voices of your cousins as they were already pouring Sand Mountain sorghum on their hot biscuits and you felt blessed to be alive and to be at Grandma's house and to know that "The Choosing" was over again for at least a week or more.

73

As adults, I don't think any of us were scarred by "The Choosing," but we were certainly all changed by it. We all live in air conditioned houses where the thermostats are always set lower than normal. We're all a bit claustrophobic though to differing degrees. We've all had weird relationship moments when someone would say, "time for bed," and we would break out into a cold sweat while running to the nearest closet or lie prone and motionless on the floor. On the positive side, we returned to school with a new perspective about games that required choosing sides. It didn't feel so bad not to be chosen first or second or third or fourth or even last. Sometimes being last gives you more time to fill your lungs, more time to look around and appreciate things, especially those that are moving. Just don't show any of us a goose. Just writing the word makes me want to hide behind the nearest chair.

The Blue Hole

I come from a long line of sweaters, not the argyle kind, nor the cotton blend nor even the more high falootin mohair (although there is one strangely unattractive one, designed for skiers with poor taste in clothing, that is documented in pictures being passed down from an uncle to my brother and then to me). We were the ones with heavy perspiration issues that all those deodorant commercials swore they could control. At the slightest hint of heat in the air or a rise in humidity, beads of sweat would appear on our foreheads, followed soon by tiny rivulets and eventually full-out rivers. Also, as if part of the evolutionary scheme for my family, we were given oversized pores to accommodate the perpetual outpouring of sweat in the hot months or hot rooms, or when exerting ourselves at anything for more than five minutes. Also being bequeathed with thin hair didn't help, because people with thick hair can sweat and it seems to remain close to their scalps, so their "dos" remain intact. For us, even the beginning of a good sweat made the little hair we had look matted like the feathers on a baby bird just hatched.

Fortunately for us, we were also blessed with a place to swim where we could deal with the heat, the sweat and the perpetual musk that was a result thereof. As in all rural communities, places where people tended to gather for whatever reason were usually given a name. Following that tradition, our spot to swim was designated the Blue Hole. The Blue Hole was a natural dip in the bed of an otherwise shallow Limestone Creek. Though the creek was the northern border of my grandparents' farm, it wasn't until it had crossed two neighboring properties that it dipped low enough to form a swimming hole.

I always considered the name dubious. I never saw the water even remotely blue. My mother says it was so deep and clear that it stayed a bluish color. As far as deep goes, it couldn't have been more than five feet and that was after a heavy rain. The colors I saw ranged from a greenish brown to a brownish green. This was always dependent on the amount of sunshine on the day you were there. Bright sunlight caused the foliage and leaves to reflect on the water given it a greenish hue. On cloudy days the rocky bottom tended to dominate the color scheme with its variations of brown more vivid through the clean flowing water. Regardless of my critical nature, as my mother would be quick to interject, we never knew it by any other name than the Blue Hole. Now that I think of it, the Brown Hole, the Green Hole or even the Brownish Green Hole don't seem as inviting.

To get there was a bit too far to walk, so we usually went in a vehicle of some sort. For my mother and her family in the earlier days this would probably have been a wagon. When we were taken as kids, it was usually a truck or car. Later, when we got older, we could ride our bikes. From the main road you traveled a field road that looped around one field, crossed through a tree line and then ran along the northern border of another field. The entry to the Blue Hole would not have been discernible to anyone who hadn't been there before. We learned to recognize it by the types of trees that grew on the embankment that led down to the creek. It was a quick trip from the main road when the field road was in good shape. You could drive your vehicle and park right at the entryway. As the field road became more rutted over the years, we had to park on the side of the main road and walk. On our bikes we could circumvent a good twenty minutes of walking time.

There were unspoken rules for the use of the swimming hole when my mother was young. Men and women did not swim at the same time. It had nothing to do with women's rights, men's rights or even the Blue Hole's rights if swimming holes have rights. For what swimming holes have to witness and endure, they probably should. But how would they pay their lawyers? Rocks, moss? Anyway, it was more of a morality issue for the men and women. Most of the men swam in the nude. According to my mother, the women swam in some sort of attire that was probably their underwear or some piece of clothing not worthy of wearing in public any longer. Because of the men's proclivity to swim au naturel, my mother and her sisters were always accompanied by their father or one of their brothers. This served two purposes. The male escort could go ahead to ensure that the creek wasn't in use at the time by workers from the neighboring fields, and if the creek was free for them, stand guard to guarantee their privacy.

Following these rules would have indeed protected them if my mother and her sisters had not been overly curious or precocious. Even though they heard splashing noises well before they got to the creek one day, and in total disregard to their father's warning from ahead that the creek was in use, they pushed through the surrounding foliage to behold the Blue Hole filled with several men from around the area. When the men heard the female giggles, they bolted from the water of the creek and dashed into the bushes on the far bank. According to mother, she had never seen a scrawnier group of naked men in her life. This makes me wonder how many naked men she had seen before. It also calls into question how much of the men she and her sisters saw. The Blue Hole was always icy cold since the creek that formed it was fed by numerous freshwater springs. Therefore, as any male who has swam in cold water will attest, there would have been very little dangling from the naked men as they ran. In her retelling of the incident she also had to cast aspersions on the men's intelligence. After all, according to her, anyone with sense would have remained in the creek where the water could cover their most private parts. In the end, she and her sisters were told to return to the field while the men dressed and left, no doubt a bit sheepishly, and harboring the knowledge that their shortcomings that weren't truly shortcomings had been revealed. And the final naked reality of the situation was that my mother and her sisters then had the Blue Hole to themselves for the rest of the afternoon.

As for my brothers, cousins and me, the Blue Hole was a magical pool, a place to prove our growing prowess and at times a pool of unadulterated adolescent fear. Accompanied by an uncle, or uncles and our father, we were often subjected to shenanigans and horror stories that I still ponder what their true intent was. If I give them the benefit of the doubt, it was all in good fun, meant to make us stronger men when we grew up, and to teach us to survive were we ever to be dropped in a jungle miles from civilization with only a shoelace or dental floss. But the things that still to this day warp my psyche, come after the good things I remember.

On the hottest of days we would weave through the tree line and the ground brush to discover the winding creek that spoke to us with gurgling words. The sun that filtered in through the tree limbs formed patterns of light that glistened and shone on the water. And if this were not magical enough, in the middle beckoned the deepest bed of the creek, the Blue Hole. When we waded into the water, the sheer iciness of it would cause us to gasp and shiver. But the deeper we got, the cold would start to wash the heat from our skin and cause us for a brief delicious moment to close our eyes as if it was almost too much to bear.

Suddenly, our eyes opened and we came to life and turned into tadpoles and fish. Then we'd leave the creek and jump from rocks again and again, each time increasing the level of difficulty of the twists and turns of our bodies before entering the water. There were splash wars and deep dive competitions. We would have looked like future Olympic swimmers if we had not been dressed in old worn out shorts and cutoff pants. It wasn't like we didn't have swimsuits. Those were at home in a drawer and saved for the remote chance that we might at some crazy point during the summer get to go to a real swimming pool. "Creeks can put a stain in things that I can't get out," our mother would inform us as if she were a spokesperson for a Tide detergent. At least we were better suited than our uncles who sometimes didn't intend to swim, but then decided it was too hot not to and ended up stripping to their underwear. From a distance, one would think they were nude as their skin that never saw the light of day tended to blend so well with the white briefs they wore.

There was something in this idyllic setting that frightened us without our uncle's help, snakes. It was their domain after all. We were the interlopers that disrupted their normally tranquil setting. If we could see them swimming on top or their heads bobbing on top of the water, we could clear the creek and allow them to go on their merry ways down stream, or up stream or really wherever they liked. After our heart rates lowered from what would have been stroke level if we had been adults, we would gingerly reenter the creek and then splash like maniacs as if just making an inordinate amount of noise would impede them from their natural courses. It would seem to work for a while. Then we would get caught up in our water aerobics and games, and suddenly out of nowhere and heading right for you, you would spot a small head with two beady eyes that seemed to have your face imprinted on them.

This is where our uncles entered in to take it from a scary fairy tale to something out of a slasher movie. One uncle would turn to another and nonchalantly mention after spitting the juice from his chewing tobacco, "I hope they know it's not the ones on top of the water they need to worry about." At this point with this new knowledge stuck in our brains like cockleburs, we became overly sensitive to anything under the water that touched our legs or feet. Even a grazing of one of our own feet against the other leg would send us shrieking to the bank. If this were not enough, the uncles would wait until we were poised to jump from the top of one of the rocks or even from the bank and reiterate a story we had heard before, but had buried deep within our psyches to minimize the damage already done the first time we heard it. "H (a nickname they often used with our father), you remember that fellow that died in the creek? You know, the one who jumped in and landed in a bed of snakes? They said he came up with snakes hanging all over him biting him again and again. Mercifully, he didn't last long enough to scream too much. I guess the snake venom was so strong that it took him out pretty quickly." It would be cleverly timed so you would hear the part about the bed of snakes as you launched into the air and then the part about the venom as you entered the water. We didn't just emerge from the water. We jettisoned ourselves like porpoises in a "Sea World" show to land, regardless of the distance, on the bank of the creek.

Although it has been many years since I've been, I'm sure the Blue Hole is still there. Though the land and the fields and even the course of the creek have changed many times through the years, I am certain I could still find it. Yet every time I commit to go, there is a hesitancy or fear that stops me. It is not the fear of the snakes that have no doubt continued to live there, even though in that adolescent part of my brain I am sure the knowledge of me has been passed down in their serpentine history, so there is at least one waiting for my return with some serious payback in mind. It is the fear that it will not be how I remember it. I do not wish to see it grown over or diminished in size. I need for it to always be the dubiously blue color my mother saw when she was a girl, to be the place where I heard my uncles and father chuckling as they launched us like missiles into the middle of it while assuring us that it was the way they learned to swim, and also to be the scene of mayhem with my brothers and cousins frantically scurrying to the banks to avoid even the smallest of snakes swimming through. As long as I don't go, it will always remain so and the many people that have passed will still be there in its icy spring fed water that washed away the heat, the sweat, the musk and even the smallest worries of the day.

Shock Theater

Dark room, flashlight pointed at the bottom of a chin, gravelly voice, eerie music and we were already nervous wrecks even before the movie began. This was Saturday night in Toney, Alabama and *Shock Theater* was on TV. Though it terrified my older brothers and me, I don't think we ever missed it. And if any of our cousins were in town, they too were subjected to the terror. We couldn't stop ourselves. Surprisingly, no parents seemed to object, even though they dealt with our nightmares for months after we'd viewed certain episodes. Heck, just writing this has gotten me a bit shaky.

First of all, we lived in a house my parents had built on the same road where my grandmother, one aunt and one uncle lived. It was a dirt road that was later graveled. It wasn't paved until years later. There were only a total of six houses on the road at the time and long stretches between most of them. There was nothing on the opposite side of the road but woods. Behind all of the houses were large crop fields and then more woods. It was the perfect area for aliens to land. They could have abducted all the residents on the road, subjected them to the most horrific experiments, which according to my mother's family had to include at least getting hit on the head, and no one would have known for days or even weeks. Now that I think about it and considering our looks, lack of common sense and sometimes questionable intelligence, there is a great possibility the aliens did land, and subsequently erased our knowledge of the event with the dreaded tap on the noggin.

The setting is further enhanced by the fact that the eastern end of the road began in a swamp, a swamp fed by a natural spring that is purported to have no bottom. I know this from the thousands of times we were either taken there or walked as a group and leaned in as closely as we could trying to see through the murkiness and find anything to signal a bottom. If adults were with us, they would shake their heads while telling us to keep on looking because you're not going to find one. If we still seemed unimpressed, we were told about the wagon pulled by two horses that had gone into the spring and never came out. If our young minds didn't appear scarred enough by this information, they resorted to scientific fact, although never corroborated by any news service we could find. A scuba diver had been hired to investigate. He never found the bottom nor any sign of the horses and wagon, and actually left with strange tics he didn't have before diving into the abyss. This knowledge, accompanied by our isolation, only compounded any irrational fears we had already manufactured in our adolescent brains.

In addition, as if we needed an extra push toward the heebie-jeebies, even closer to our house in the woods about a mile to the northwest was an old family cemetery. It was perched on the lip of a hill just before the land gave way to a steep drop into a marsh-like area that was fed by a creek. A smell of decay wafted up in a perpetual slight breeze that caused the trees to flutter. The markers for the graves were gone, but you could walk in the area and all of a sudden feel the ground give way and drop into the rectangular sinkholes where the graves were located. It is difficult to describe your emotions as a kid when you realized you were standing, sitting or lying in a grave. If that were not enough, the others along for the walk got to see you rise up from the grave you had stumbled into, scratched head to toe from the numerous brambles and vines encountered on the way to the cemetery, and resembling what we imagined someone who had been buried for eons must look like. It is a miracle that no one was hurt in our mad scrambles to exit the area. Our horn-rimmed glasses somehow stayed on our noses though our eyes had increased in size at least tenfold. It was also our first time to experience a cardio workout. Our parents loved every minute of it. I think they took the adage that "whatever doesn't kill you makes you stronger" too literally. Their only worry was whether or not our underwear was still clean. What they didn't know was that some of us were going commando for the first time. Our drawers were still in the cemetery, pristine and white just as they were before we ran out of them.

The place that we gathered to watch *Shock Theater* was a strange room. It had originally been a carport, but our dad on one of his building sprees had decided to enclose it and make it a den. There were things he didn't complete. The original concrete steps were left as access from the house into the room. Also, a window in the bedroom my oldest brother and I shared was never walled up. So we could pull back a curtain and look into the den. The floor was the original concrete. I think they did put down linoleum, but the floor remained hard and cold. The furniture was a hodgepodge of items, odd shaped bookshelves our father built, a patio lounge chair where our mother usually sat, and the hardest brown naugahyde vinyl couch ever constructed. Our father also had a chair, but for the life of me I don't remember how it looked.

It was the couch or the floor where my brothers and guests usually resided. Fortunately for us, the couch folded down into a bed that provided enough room for a bunch of frightened kids. It didn't matter where anyone was sitting in the room. When *Shock Theater* came on the TV, one by one all viewers would migrate, sometimes slowly and at others in mad dashes, until we all ended up on that rock hard couch with blankets or quilts over our heads, even on the hottest nights of summer. Come to think of it, we would have been an excellent prototype for the monster in *The Blob* when it was made years later.

There was no blood or guts in the *Shock Theater* movies we watched. Everything was black and white and full of shadowy figures. All the horrible things seemed to be implied, or so well suggested, that our minds took over and imagined the grisliest scenarios to unfold. Dracula, Frankenstein and the Wolfman entered our brains and our nightmares. After watching one of the movies, I remember only feeling safe enough to sleep if my body was fully covered. Any appendage that slipped out from under the covers was prime game for Dracula to grab or bite.

One time my parents had to come to my bedroom I was screaming at such a feverish pitch. They said I told them there were giant rats on the end of my bed. This is after watching a movie about mutant rats that were as large as dogs and hungry for human flesh. People could only move safely under the cover of metal garbage cans and they could hear the claws of the shrews, the mutant rats, scratching against the metal trying to make them a meal. I recently looked up that movie. It turns out the rats were dogs they had covered in animal hides. I told my dog, Freckles, "Don't even think about it."

My middle brother told me *Shock Theater* was the reason I shared a bedroom with my oldest brother. After an especially horrific episode in which the monster lived in a mirror, my oldest brother refused to enter the bedroom alone. It seems that there was a mirror on the dresser in the room. To resolve the problem our parents made me his bedmate. Looking back, this seems a strange choice of actions, since I was four years younger and much scrawnier than he was. In addition, how could I protect him from a monster in the mirror when I was so busy hiding under the covers from Dracula and the shrews?

DON'T TELL ALL YOUR BUSINESS!

There were added issues when our cousins were there for a visit. When the movies ended, everyone was too scared to walk the road back to Grandma's house, and even after being driven there by an adult, they then had to sleep in a house that had a commanding view of the swamp to the east and the bottomless spring. Since there was no air conditioning, the windows and front door had to remain open all night. As any true *Shock Theater* enthusiast knew, Dracula could become a mist and easily pass through Grandma's screen door. In addition, the swamp sounds they must have heard are mind-boggling to me. Was that last sound the Wolfman leaving the swamp and climbing the hill? Was the bottomless spring where the swamp monster hid during the day? Did the rats in the barn mutate to become shrews? Not even Grandma's snores could have provided solace for them. I would have commiserated more with them if I had been able to remove my terrified brain and body from under my cocoon of covers.

Looking back, I can understand why we were such easy prey for movies that never showed blood and guts. Beyond our location in the outskirts of nowhere and all the stories our parents told us, we had vivid imaginations. It is how we survived growing up in rural areas without many toys to play with. We spent days inventing our own worlds and ways to have fun. So when the horror movies made the slightest suggestion of pending slaughters or ghastly monsters that hid in the dark, we were ready to believe their existence. I would hold up any of these early movies against all the slasher movies made today. I venture to say if Michael Myers or Freddy Krueger had grown up like we did, they would have been so busy dodging mirrors and hiding under the covers to keep Dracula from biting some part of their bodies, they wouldn't have had time to slash anyone.

I have just reached an age when I can allow a foot or hand to dangle outside the covers. But having written this, I'll probably reconsider that tonight and maybe even climb into a sleeping bag. There will be no open windows and I may even hang a sign outside that says, "Visitors Not Welcome." What about that, Dracula? I won't enter a room where a mirror is located without first turning on the lights, or maybe I'll empty the linen closet to cover them all. As for the huge mutant rats, I really have no strategy. But just in case, I'll leave Shakespeare's "Taming of the Shrew" on my night stand.

The Ice House

I don't remember my parents having verbal arguments when I was growing up. My dad was generally passive unless pushed to a breaking point and he only seemed to reach that point while watching my middle brother play basketball. His adamant disagreements with the referees' calls often found him threatened with either technical fouls or ejection from the games. My mother, on the other hand, was passive aggressive, but that was only with my father. She would become sullen and non-responsive to him if she were truly upset. With others, including my brothers and me, you can drop the passive part.

We rarely saw them in contentious situations when we were younger. I think it was because they were so busy. After attending college on the GI Bill, my dad had secured a job on the arsenal. I think he earned a fairly good wage, but still had to work overtime to pay the bills. In addition to maintaining the household and raising my two brothers and me, for a couple of years my mother worked in the cotton fields for six or seven weeks, or for as long as it took to get the crop in. My brothers were old enough to join her with sacks on their backs from early morning to dusk. I was fortunate in that I was too young to really pick enough to matter. I did have a flour sack with a strap sewn on it that I pretty much played with until I grew tired of it, which usually didn't take that long. Then I could either ride on my mother's sack as she pulled it down the rows or climb into the cotton wagon and nap. At the end of the long days in the field, we would return home and Mother would prepare supper for us all. During these times I think my parents were too tired to disagree.

Things got better when I was old enough to start school. It allowed Mother to substitute teach at the school that my brothers and I attended. What she earned, in addition to my dad's salary with overtime, was enough to eliminate the cotton picking gigs. To be honest, I kind of missed it. My brothers did not. This did not mean that Mother was more idle. She made her own clothes so that extra money was available to buy clothes for my brothers and me. She also kept the most meticulous house which in itself is amazing, considering she was raising three boys. Nothing was ever out of place. Her wood floors were always so polished that you could see a reflection of yourself as you walked across them. My brothers and I were programmed from an early age to help with her daily regime of maintenance, and it wasn't all bad. When the floors were waxed, at least twice a month, it was our job to don several pairs of old socks and slide over them again and again as if we were ice skaters. When she could see herself in the reflection like she was posed in a picture, the rink was closed.

Things were so good at one time there was enough money for her to pay a lady from the neighborhood to come in and do the ironing for her. For Mother, everything had to be ironed. Everything in its place and anything washed wrinkle free and starched. There were no dryers with fancy chemical-coated sheets to throw in to battle the wrinkles. There was a washer, clothesline and an ironing board that was always set up in the utility room. All our clothes were cotton, the fabric that seems to send out invitations to wrinkles from miles around. What I didn't know at the time was that this almost obsessive need for order and control would lend itself to a critical nature when dealing with things she couldn't completely control, like my dad.

Perhaps, if they had had a few extremely loud verbal battles they could have gotten past their differences more quickly. Maybe, if things had not gotten easier, there would have been less time for her to notice and even point out his imperfections. But it was as if they were riding on a bus together and one day the bus stopped at the wrong stop. When they disembarked, the proclivity to disagree was waiting for them like a piece of luggage someone had forgotten and left behind. It would be my guess that she was the one to pick it up. It was a finders keepers with a no return policy. It was theirs for the rest of their marriage.

My brothers and I were always aware when they were at odds. They spent inordinate amounts of time in their separate areas of comfort. For our mother it was the house. For our dad it was his shop and the yard. We would find our dad tilling the already tilled garden. If questioned, he would offer that there were still too many large clumps that would impede the planting. Mother could be found with a washcloth, cleaning the salt and pepper shakers in her collection, often forgetting where she had started and as a result cleaning some of them more than once.

We didn't always know what caused the sour feelings to arise. At other times we were well aware. Our dad may have forgotten to bring something home she had requested. He had failed to notice the new dress she had made and was wearing. Perhaps for her the most egregious crime he could commit was to either disagree with her on just about anything or worse yet dismiss her opinion or complaint in a joking manner. When the latter happened, my brothers and I knew to disappear until we could assess the extent of the fallout to come.

Even in the middle of one of their rows, we didn't really notice any difference in our dad. We could tell he was bothered and a little less vocal. But he still talked to us as if all was normal. He would intone mother's name occasionally while shaking his head and hammering a nail with a bit more force than usual, but otherwise he seemed the same. There was the sometimes, "What's got into your Mother?" But I don't think he ever expected a response. I guess it was his passive nature.

With our mother, it was totally different. There was an icy feeling in the house when you entered. Mother would be eerily quiet as if she were living in a sack of cotton she once picked. She would be so intent on whatever task that was at hand that often we weren't sure she knew we were home. Sometimes she became this way not as a result of something that had just happened. It was as if she stored some hard feelings away, and later when she had more time to examine them, she took them out and picked away any good things that might have been attached and then squeezed the bad that was left until it became as hard as a rock. When we saw her going to this place of anger, my brothers and I could often alert our dad by catching him as he got out of the car. The looks on our faces signaled that she was in one of her moods as he called them. He would go out to his shop and piddle until supper necessitated all of us to gather at the kitchen table.

There was one thing I discovered that seemed to epitomize my dad's passive approach to their disagreements or Mother's intense moods. It was an innocent discovery for an inquisitive country boy playing in his father's shop. A commode seat with lid was hanging on one of the side walls. I climbed up on the workbench to reach it. When I lifted the lid I found a crude drawing of my mother done with either red paint or a marker. There was no mistaking that it was her. He had added prominent frown lines to her forehead and given her eyes an unmistakable malice. Underneath her picture he had written, "Aggie," a name I knew she hated to be called. I lowered the lid quickly, knowing it was something private. On those days when things were at their worst and he had retreated to his shop, I'm sure he lifted that lid and found some satisfaction as he worked away his frustration and unease.

I guess it was inevitable that Mother would become aware of my brothers and me forewarning our dad about her moods. On one occasion, she was ready for us. I was around eight or nine years old, putting my brothers at around twelve and thirteen. We were at the supper table waiting for our dad to get home from work. It was our parents' anniversary and our mother had instructed us to not mention it to our dad. We were not comfortable in the roles of co-conspirators. Not only did we not want to betray our father, we also knew this was not going to end well. If one of us even looked like we might rise from the table, she would affix her laser look on us. There was nothing remotely passive about it. It was a look that let us know how unpleasant she could make our lives. It was a look that could put the wrinkles back into our clothes that had been starched and ironed. For the most part, we didn't even look at each other. We kept our heads down and focused on our plates with the slices of meatloaf with ketchup on top, the great northern beans and the spinach we all hated. All of it should have had a thin layer of ice forming on top. If we had been able to breathe, I'm sure we would have produced icy vapors.

So, after long enough for God to have created a whole other universe with so many species that Darwin's head would have burst, Daddy arrived and took his place at the table. I don't know if he noticed that the minute bits of conversation from Mother were directed only to my brothers and me. If he addressed her, she didn't respond. The meal felt like a last supper with my brothers and me stealing glances at each other. We kept our heads down for the most part, fearful that we might get caught in our mother's cross hairs, or worse yet, somehow signal our father that we were keeping a secret and as a result suffer our mother's wrath as a consequence. In our trancelike states, forks full of the much-dreaded spinach often found their way into our mouths and settled in for the long haul. Even our gag reflexes were put on hold, and eventually any further eating was impossible. When Mother finished eating she stood up, picked up her plate and glass and took them to the sink. She came back, pushed her chair in and left the kitchen. We could hear her footsteps through the hallway and then the sound of their bedroom door as it shut.

When he asked us what was going on, all we could do was shrug. He got up, walked to their bedroom, opened the door and asked her what was wrong. A cold icy air blew past him down the hall and into the kitchen where my brothers and I still sat with the spinach that had now become closer to cud lodged in our mouths. There was no answer from the darkened room. He came back to the kitchen and said that it appeared our mother had gone to bed. It was a quarter of six in the evening. He shook his head and his shoulders seemed to slump as he went out the back door to his shop.

It wasn't until a couple of days later that she confronted him with the fact that he had forgotten their anniversary. It had been a cold, cold house for those two long days. I learned then that my mother was capable of holding on to things regardless of who was hurt by them. It would be the first of many times that she shut doors on my father, and she would do the same with other people that she removed from her life. I'm sure my dad spent much of those two days in his shop with the commode lid up.

On my bedroom wall I have a picture of my parents and me. It was taken when we were visiting my mother's relatives on Sand Mountain. I must have been around three years old at the time which would mean that Mother was 27 and my dad was 31. There is a strange play of shadows and light in the picture with the shadows almost obscuring the clapboard house behind us, except for one of its walls with a window and a row of posts that support the front porch. The light seems to focus most on the three of us. My dad's face appears to emerge from the shadows. My mother's is fully illuminated, but her dark sweater is lost in the recess of the porch. I seem to be in the direct sunlight as my right hand is up shielding my face and my image is so bright that I seem to be glowing. In my left hand is a half eaten apple and the red of the uneaten part sharply contrasts with the blacks, grays and browns that dominate the picture. My dad is young and handsome and is looking directly at the camera. He is wearing what appears to be a light colored sports coat, maybe blue or gray and darker colored pleated trousers with a narrow tan belt threaded through the loops. His left hand holds a pipe to his smiling lips and the smile causes a dimple on the right side of his face. His right arm is around my mother and appears to be pulling her closer to him with the close contact causing that side of his jacket to rise and bunch up where their bodies connect. My mother is young, pretty and stylish in her short dark sweater, a brownish colored pencil skirt and open toed shoes. One of her hands appears to rest on my dad's side while the other arm is clutching his back. Instead of looking at the camera, her broad smiling gaze is focused on me. It was taken a long time before the ice age. It is how I choose to remember them.

Corncob Wars

For all of those school officials who in their infinite and sometimes circumspect wisdom deemed the game of dodge ball to be too dangerous for kids to play at school, I offer a more dangerous game that we often played when I was growing up, and survived without permanent damage, although this might be a point of debate since some of us ended up without good running-around sense. We called it Corncob War. It was not sanctioned by the government or any health organization, and was not overseen by any written rules. It was allowed by our parents with one stipulation: if anyone came crying to our grandmother's house, then that day the game was ended. You could appear later with dry, caked blood over two-thirds of your body and nothing was said. The fear of a lost eye was not a factor since everyone wore glasses. If a more serious injury occurred without the shedding of tears, say a broken bone or a concussion, then that person simply sat out. Any medical intervention on the day of the injury was out of the question, as it would have necessitated one of the aunts leaving the dinner table or an uncle having to miss out on a couple of beers.

Our game or war always took place in our grandmother's barn. It was a large weathered wood structure with a large main drive bay, two somewhat smaller drive bays on either side, several interior stalls including a feed room and above it all a large loft. In the old feed room was where most of the remnants of the corn were found; the ammo stockpile the Navy Seals would target to abort any possible terrorist corncob threats to national security.

To begin we would choose teams, an often long and laborious process that always included hot debates, as there were cousins who were either not as quick as the others, more prone to crying when struck by a cob weathered to the point of being rock-like or whose prescription lenses were so thick that their aim was impaired as much as their vision. When teams were finally decided, a stockpile of corncobs were shoved into pockets, hats, loose shirts, and for the truly wizened veterans, old burlap bags. Teams then raced to establish strategic home bases. Although the loft would have seemed to be the best choice due to its access for attack from a variety of vantage points, it was also home to one of the largest rat snakes known to mankind. It was bigger around than the largest cousin's calf muscle. That probably is not a good descriptive, since not only were we visually impaired, but also had inherited skinny legs with knobby knees and the largest cousin's calf muscle was about the size of a little league baseball bat. It didn't matter. We knew the snake was there somewhere. We had seen it, usually with the guidance of our grandfather after we had been playing in the loft for hours, creating idyllic worlds where all was well and everyone was brave and nice looking. He would climb up the ladder and stick his head into the loft and state, "Now, don't y'all upset my snake." Then he would chuckle and point to a rafter over our heads where we could see the body of the serpent weaving a good 8 to 9 feet around the support joists. He didn't have to worry. We always deserted Camelot immediately. We made no apologies to King Arthur. We figured he had a sword and could take care of himself. So, the loft was never a base. Brave teams would dash through it for quick assaults, but never linger. After all, with our looks, we probably didn't appear much different than the snake's usual and obviously frequent meal.

Once home bases were set, the war began. The ultimate goal was to pelt other team members with as many corncobs as possible, while not being hit. Different strategies were employed to reach that goal. If a team was fast, they would dart back and forth in and out of stalls and bins, drawing fire until the other team exhausted their supply of cobs and then pound them with their own as they attempted to reach the supply stall. Teams with strong arms would launch attacks on other team's home bases, hammering them incessantly until they raced out of Dodge City, relinquishing their stockpiles. Perhaps the best strategy was to leave one member of the team to guard home base while other members went on assault missions. In the end, corncob war really involved a lot of yelling, running, hiding, and bluffing with clever lines like, "oh heck, wish I wasn't out of cobs" or "did the snake just slither into that stall?" or even the lowest, "you shouldn't have thrown so hard, cause she's going to the house and now you're going to get it." The latter led to moans and groans and a complete collapse of all defenses for the team that had believed the taunt. That made them victims to an all-out assault and the accursed words, "And this is what you get!"

As for the battles themselves, their duration was always impacted by several factors. Loss of interest was a biggie. If there was too much time spent planning strategies as opposed to actual action, then some teams would wander off to find other entertainment like catching crawdads in the creek. Sometimes, the bigger and a bit more sadistic cousins would become kamikazes and go on assaults with the intent of maiming the more innocent and docile cousins who would then refuse to play anymore. Finally, if someone reached into one of the bins where the corncobs were located and touched one of the many rats that still lived there, the war was over, as they had to return to the house and change their soiled undies.

There were epic battles from time-to-time, usually when friends were over or all the cousins were visiting at the same time. It is difficult to assign a time frame to them, because we became so lost in the wars that time seemed to disappear. The smell of the old barn wood, hay and the remnants of manure from the animals once housed there were intoxicating. The flashes of clothes, the snippets of heads or someone's leg or arm as they disappeared around a corner or into a stall became hypnotic. There was no rhythm to our breathing as we were either hidden behind a stall door and forcing our breathing to be shallow and soft so we didn't give away our position, or sucking down huge gulps of air with our hearts racing as we darted through the maze of the barn trying to elude the multiple corncobs that were being hurled at us in that moment. We moved with stealth and sometimes reckless abandon. The outside world no longer existed. It was us and the barn. It was the rough feel of corncobs clutched in our hands. It was the excitement generated when your arm drew back and then shot forward to throw a cob. It was an intense feel of relief as you felt the air stir as a corncob narrowly missed you. On those days, during the epic battles, we achieved the ultimate goal for kids by getting lost in a world of our own making.

For those who might think us a tad barbaric, even when thrown by the biggest and meanest cousin, a corncob blow was not that bad. It could sting and occasionally remove small sections of skin. The result of the hardest throw could leave the imprint of the cob on your arm or leg. It was a honeycomb-like pattern before the bruising set in and became a cool battle scar that was better than a tattoo. Most injuries or wounds were never noticed until much later when the war was over and even then it was more of an aside and a bafflement as to when and how it had happened. We never aimed at someone's face, not because it might do some serious irreparable harm, but for fear of breaking their glasses. For that offense we would be lectured for days about how hard our parents worked and how ungrateful we were and how good we had it, unlike them.

It never dawned on us at the time that we were not the first to battle with corncobs in that barn. My mother and her siblings had done the same when they weren't encumbered with the many chores they had to do. As we raced and hid and threw and squealed, there was a vestige of them as kids always with us. Maybe at times they were following us to see where we would go. At others perhaps, we were following them without knowing it, as if our battle routes were predestined. We had much more in common than we knew. We had all fought in and survived corncob wars.

Before the barn finally gave in to age and decay and had to be torn down, I had the opportunity to revisit it many times. It was always like reconnecting with an old friend. As I wandered through it, I passed through spaces where there was the imprint of intense joy. I could see the eyes of an uncle or cousin peering through the slats of a stall. I could hear a scampering of feet in the loft above me and a muffling of excited voices. There was a whistling sound and I felt a brief burst of air as if a corncob had passed by my head. As I opened stall doors, there were intakes of breath as if I had stumbled on the hiding places of some of the combatants. When I climbed the ladder into the loft, I felt the same apprehension I did as a kid even though I knew the rat snake had to have died years ago. Occasionally, on the hardened clay floors in the remnants of straw I would find corncobs. When I picked them up, it was as if I was eleven years old again. I stuffed all but one into my pockets. I clutched the remaining corncob in my right hand, feeling the roughness pushing a beehive-like pattern into my palm, and I was ready for battle.

Scaly Barks and Crawdads

Though the title may lead you to believe this is about an app for a smart phone, tablet or computer, it is set in a time that came decades before they even existed. The phones then were either on a wall, a specially made phone bench, a table next to an easy chair or in some cases the kitchen counter. And all such phones were connected to a squirrelly cord. Those cords seemed to have lives of their own in their unpredictability. In a period of seconds they could somehow tangle into a series of puzzle-worthy knots and that was without the user altering his or her stance or position in any way. In addition, the use of the phones was limited. We were all on eight party lines. So unless it was an emergency in which you interjected yourself into an ongoing conversation to scream, "There's a rabid dog in my yard," you had to wait your turn. Sometimes, the wait was short because you could hear when someone else had picked up and it was the courteous thing for the ones on-line to wrap up their business and allow you access. Other times it could be a long stretch like when Hilda Mae was receiving step-by-step directions on how to make a dress for the Sunday church social from her mother, Big Mama Mae, who could only explain it by making a dress herself at the same time on the other end of the line. As kids, none of this really mattered because the phones were really adult things only relinquished to us to call a friend on rare occasions and even then under intense adult scrutiny.

But this is not about apps or phones. It is about nature, scaly barks, the nuts from hickory trees and crawdads, small critters that lived in the creeks and rare special days with family. To hear scaly barks and crawdads spoken in a single sentence by one of the adult family members could only mean one of our at least twice a year adventures to the western end of the Howard's farm. It was there that the Limestone Creek meandered through their wooded acreage, and it was there along its banks that many hickory trees that produced the scaly bark nuts, or as we had always known them as simply scaly barks, grew in abundance. As if life couldn't get any better for us, the creek next to the trees was wide, mostly shallow and perfect for fishing for crawdads.

So in late summer or early fall, one aunt would call the other when the phone line was open due to Big Mae and Little Mae being finished with their sewing projects, and set the adventure in motion. We would gather at our grandmother's house for an operational meeting. How many were going? There were usually two to three aunts, my two brothers and me, several cousins and occasionally a few friends. How many vehicles did we need for transport? It usually took three with the adults seated comfortably in the front and the kids crammed into the back like Vienna sausages in a can. The vehicles were necessary, because even though the Howard's farm was only three or four miles away, walking there would take up too much of the day. Next, our clothing would have to be inspected to make sure we weren't wearing anything that couldn't be ruined in Lord knows what kind of situation we'd face. Were we wearing shoes that would work on both dry land and in the creek? Though the bottoms of our feet by the end of the summer were tougher than rawhide, one of the aunts would point out how sharp the rocks were in the creek, that there were razor-like barbs hidden in the leaves on the ground in the woods and then while surveying us like we were members of a chain gang, profess as her eyebrows rose up like Venetian blinds, that she would not be carrying anyone out. Then, as if they were a pro wrestling tag team, another aunt would take over to drill us on snake avoidance procedures. Inevitably, the previous prison guard aunt would remind us, snakebite or no snakebite, she would not be carrying us out. After what felt like a day of hard labor building a road through a swamp, we would load up and be on our way.

The last mile of the trip to the Howard's farm was like riding a roller coaster. We turned on a gravel road at the top of a hill and then dipped and turned, rose once more only to dip and spiral until we finally hit the flat area where the farm was located. We were always slightly dizzy Viennas when we caught sight of the planted fields that lay on the left side of the road. To the right were heavy woods that blocked any views of the creek that ran there. At the end on the left was the dogtrot house where the Howards lived. Actually, it wasn't really the end of the road, but the place we parked our vehicles. Remnants of the road continued downward to the creek, crossed it at one point and some semblance of it could still be seen covered with undergrowth and ferns until it disappeared into the woods. It had at one time been part of a main travel route between Pulaski, Tennessee and Huntsville. As kids, we rarely processed the historical information the adults shared at such times. All we knew was that the road gave clear and easy access to the creek. After all, we weren't on an educational school trip for gosh sake. Come to think of it, we didn't even have school field trips back then.

The only thing that blocked us from an all-out charge to the creek, other than the aunt's laser beam looks to the backs of our heads, was the occasional presence of one or all of the Howards on the porch of their house or in the yard. Under those conditions we were required to wait while the aunts exchanged pleasantries with them. They were an interesting family. There were two bachelor brothers and a spinster sister that lived in the house. They had lived on their farm longer than my grandparents had lived on theirs. They were considered to be good family friends although they weren't known for socializing much. I guess you can't marry if you never go anywhere to meet someone. Their house always caught our attention though mainly because it was so rare to see a house built that way. If we hadn't had scaly barks, crawdads and the creek swirling around in our heads we might have learned that there was a purpose for the breezeway down the middle with sleeping quarters to one side and the kitchen and eating area to the other. But all we caught was the term "dogtrot" and in our slightly off adolescent intelligence, shook our heads in wonder that their dogs didn't even have to circle the house to get from the back yard to the front.

Our ears were almost batlike they were so attuned to the conversation of the adults. We were gauging the length of their pauses and the change in the lilt of their voices. The word "well" would cause our muscles to tense. It was those moments that we never appreciated enough, when something wonderful was just beyond our reach and in the hesitation it magnified to become bigger and more special, when even your breathing became more than you could bear. Just at the point when you thought you couldn't stand it for one second more, the adults would conclude their conversation and signal you could go. We would race down the road toward the creek, shrieking so loudly as we went that we could barely hear the aunts screaming, "Watch for snakes!"

Our journey through the creek was loud and boisterous. Any snakes in our path would be well aware of our approach long before we got anywhere near them. Splashing was allowed as long as it didn't involve the aunts who often took advantage of the rule by splashing us with zeal when we least expected it. The farther we waded the less authoritative the aunts seemed to become as if they were remembering the kids they used to be when wandering the creek with their siblings or parents. There were parts of it that were special to all of us, whether it was the calming canopy of the trees along the bank, the sound of the creek as it flowed in its decades-long path, or the wildlife that appeared to check out the source of the ruckus that so rudely broached the normal sounds of the woods. For me, it was always the rocks. The colors, the feel of them like the smoothness of the ones that had been altered by the flow of the water and the rough edges of the others that had somehow evaded it. I could hold them and sense a life in them and a history and imagine all the things they had witnessed. In this way, with each of us in our own and sometimes collective revelries, we would arrive at the spot where the hickory trees stood with what seemed to be a kajillion scaly barks scattered on the bank and in the creek beneath them.

We would select our spots to crack them, a dry spot for sitting with a large rock to crack them on and another rock to do the cracking. We looked for the ones where the hard outside husks had been split open from when they had hit the ground or rocks, or at least where the husks had been split to the point that you could pry them off without much effort. For an interminable length of time we would sit and crack them and dig out what meat we could extract with the vast majority of it falling to the ground or in the creek for the wildlife to savor when we left. So focused on the task at hand, we lost our loudness for a spell and were able to hear the natural sounds of the woods around us and the creek's soothing trickling.

It was then that our aunts would tell us stories about when they were kids and had been there before. We were more attentive, since most of the stories we had been told had been about the hard times, the "you kids don't know how good you have it" stories, the "we would have been happy to have a stick" stories, the flour sack clothes stories and the "if you only knew what we had to go through" stories. These stories were before all of those, when they were not old enough to work in the fields or at least during times they got to put their hoes or cotton sacks down for a day and enjoy themselves. They laughed a lot in the telling as if in each story they were once again back when it all happened. We were too young to appreciate what they were giving us. In those moments, there was a juncture between their childhoods and our own, a rare melding of the two. Suddenly, as if the feel of the flour sack dresses chafed their skin and brought them back to their senses, one would stand, breaking the spell and the silence and announce,"Enough of this foolishness, let's catch some crawdads."

Fishing for crawdads, or crayfish or crawfish as they are also known, was an art or skill imparted to us by our mothers and grandmother. It was not that the men didn't possess the skill. It was just that the women of the family either had the time to share it or placed more importance on it. What we were fishing for were the smaller version of the crawfish found in the ocean and served boiled in restaurants. But they had all the features of the bigger version, including the pincers and the long swishy tails. In the creeks they hid under flat rocks or in the creek bottom where there were sandy patches. Someone watching us from above might have said we looked much like them in the way we darted haphazardly from place to place, or in our momentarily motionless stances that ended abruptly in firing-on-all-cylinders dashes. Heck, we probably resembled them up close the way our glasses magnified our eyes to be more prominent as they sat on each side of our larger than normal noses. Some might have actually chosen the crawdads to be the more attractive.

So, while the aunts procured the two-prong sticks we would use to fish, we would scour the creek for the best spots to find them. It was important that the aunts find our fishing implements, because if the prongs were too long, the crawdads could escape and if they were too short, they could injure the crawdads. We were not raised to be cruel to animals or things. If something was shot or caught on a fishing line it was to be eaten. I'm not sure the study bobs (bumble bees without stingers) or the June bugs that we tied strings to their legs to create flying pets would support this and neither would the fireflies we caught, put in jars and later shook vigorously to make them light up more brightly.

We weren't aware of the idea of a universal consciousness yet, nor had we heard of Hinduism or Buddhism. Did I also say we didn't have many store-bought toys? Anyway, the aunts would supply us with the most effective and as much as possible humane fishing sticks.

The secret to successful crawdad fishing was patience and focus. This meant we had to reel in our natural inclinations to be loud and obnoxious clodhoppers. Only then would we be able to tap into our inner Zen. Our grandmother would have said that wasn't possible because there were no Chinese in our family that she knew of except for the dark haired girl with no eyelashes that our great uncle dated. Our aunts would have countered that the girl was from Mississippi and her eyelashes were burned off by a campfire after too much moonshine had been consumed. So, we would sit as still as possible as we flipped flat rocks while looking for them. The rocks had to be moved with delicate motions to both not frighten away the crawdads nor dislodge grit from the bottom that would cloud the water and hide them if they were there. If you found one that didn't dart away immediately, you'd poise your stick just above it and then quickly push down until the prongs settled just behind its head, pinning it to the bottom and allowing you to reach down and grab it. We would then hoist it out of the water and shout gleefully and pompously as if we were deep sea fishermen who had just speared a great white shark. I think the crawdads were probably more annoyed than frightened as we held them out for inspection from the group. They wiggled and attempted to get us with their tiny pincers until we released them back into the creek. We should have put tiny marks on them for identification purposes because I have no doubt some were caught more than once. As a result, we may have set into a motion an altering to their genetic code. Some of their descendants are no doubt in the creeks today with special defense mechanisms to protect them against any humans wearing glasses and possessing questionable intelligence.

Our walk back involved no splash fights, and we tended to be more clumsy, slipping in places where we had been sure-footed going in. We were a tired and sated crew. All our senses had been overloaded in a good way. We would dream about it that night and talk about all that happened for days. As we loaded back into the cars, the aunts once again assumed their prison guard personas, but it really wasn't necessary. As we squeezed in, to become the Vienna sausages in a can once again, it was as if that strange gel that enveloped the sausages and almost made you barf if a bit of it got into your mouth when eating them, was all gone. On the drive back, the only coherent and mutual thought we could muster was about our grandmother. What had she cooked for us? Please, oh please, let it be fried apple pies!

When I watch kids today as they sit motionless and fully entranced by their cell phones, tablets, computers or TVs, I am struck by the fact that all of their devices have borders or edges. There is no peripheral vision, and it is that peripheral vision that often helps us better understand where we have set our focus. It is in our peripheral vision where we often find something or someone that causes us to readjust and change our focus. It is there that a thousand magical things can happen. Books always give us peripheral vision. They signal our brains to picture things without borders or edges. Those adventures with our aunts were blessings in which there were never borders, in which our peripheral vision was always important. Our grandmother would always tell us, "Keep your eyes and ears open or you might miss something."

As a result of what they taught and gave us, I can still taste the small bits of the meat of the scaly barks in my mouth. I can still feel the wiggling crawdad held triumphantly in my hand. There are mornings when I sit on my deck drinking my coffee and watching the birds in the trees when a sudden motion in my peripheral vision causes me to turn my head in time to see two chipmunks chasing each other with crazy abandon over the rocks and through the yard and I have to catch myself before yelling, "Watch out for the snakes!"

King of the Hill

Erma Bombeck entitled one of her books, *The Grass Is Always Greener Over the Septic Tank*. Perhaps it was published too late to cue us, or maybe we were beyond being cued. After all, even though we were blessed with some degree of intelligence, we still remained clueless in so many ways. This was, and probably still is, for our own protection. Let's just call it God's way of taking care of the innocent, or as others might term us, the blissfully ignorant.

Anyway, Ms. Bombeck's book title suggested that regardless of where she grew up, she could just as easily have been raised with us in Toney, Alabama. She could have been one of the cousins or "boat people," as we referred to ourselves after viewing a multitude of pictures of us growing up. We sported crew cuts and burr cuts and ponytails

111

and poorly executed bobs. We were all wearing some variation of either black or brown horn-rimmed glasses, the kind that always set slightly askew on a variety of perpetually peeling noses. And even our noses were assigned some distinction as belonging to, or resulting from some grandiose genetic plan. They were all evidence, and as clearly distinctive as fingerprints, for our aunts and uncles and even grandparents to forever connect us to some remote family line. It was just an easier way for everyone to actually avoid pointing out the obvious, that our noses were either too big or too little or too bulbous or shaped like a lopsided mushroom or all a bit pinched and droopy from supporting the weight of the forty pound glasses we all had to wear.

In the summers, the "boat people" would gather at our grandmother's farm, not by boats of course, but by various makes of automobiles. Most of them were station wagons to accommodate the larger families. Some bore logos to advertise successful business ventures. Success at the time was measured mostly by possessions rather than accomplishments. A brand new vehicle, a boat being towed, a luggage rack sporting more than was necessary for a two-week stay and a business logo all signaled prosperity to a family that had originated from a farm on a dirt back-road. However, none of the trappings in any way could change the appearance of the passengers of any vehicles. We were all still basically "boat people." We would have looked just as at home in Cambodia, or a northern province of China or even some remote undiscovered port on a thought-to-be underpopulated region of Greenland.

Our grandmother's farm was nestled on the top of a hill with the house sitting close to a dirt road. It was flanked by a large swamp to the east at the bottom of the hill. To the north were open acres which were still farmed. Beyond the fields were woods with a creek and to the west there were homes of the family members who had not caught a boat to migrate. As "boat kids" we had free range of the farm as long as at least one of us was in close enough proximity to hear one of the aunts call us in. This wasn't often, as they were too busy eating or talking and content to have us out of their hair that was usually bound tightly in rollers. Strange, how I don't remember some of them out of those rollers. I guess it was part of their appearance, a new wave thing ahead of its time. You know, "I'll be ready to go in a minute, hon. Just let me get these rollers in my hair."

Typically, we weren't called in unless it had become very dark. We couldn't see well in the daytime and our vision through our thick glasses diminished quickly with the dissipation of natural light. We were occasionally summoned to eat whatever the adults had not consumed. The amounts left varied dependent on which aunts were present at the table. Although all were healthy eaters, one in particular seemed to be in training for a pie eating contest. Finally, we were corralled, usually only if during one of our games someone was injured and had tearfully related how it happened to the feasting Aunts/Gestapo. Punishment usually came in such incidents, in what would eventually be termed time-out. All but the whistleblowing victim would be anchored to the front porch or surrounding yard, and subjected to litanies of how someone's eye could have been put out even though we thought but never voiced how unlikely that was considering the thickness of the lenses in our glasses. Or worse someone could have been hit on the head. Although it sounded foolish at the time, it now seems more logical. After all we didn't have much sense to begin with. A blow to the head that would remove even one iota of it would have proven extremely detrimental if not catastrophic.

The "boat captains" or fathers were never present during any of these episodes. Where they went was always a mystery to us, even though we did catch snippets of conversation from the "boat wives" regarding their location. That was until one of them spotted us, at which point all conversation ceased, and laser eyes descended demanding to know the purpose of the intrusion. And it had better be because someone was hurt. If not, the interloper(s) would be subjected to front porch time-out. All we really knew was that the "boat captains" skedaddled as quickly as they could, and returned late into the evening smelling of cigarettes and beer. One time they returned with a truck bed full of unripe plums as what turned out to be a most unwelcome peace offering to their mates. But, that is another story. Then they were subjected to their own forms of time-out as dictated by their respective Gestapo wives.

Front porch time-out was really not that bad. We were quickly forgotten and could easily move into the yard surrounding the house. We were wiry and quick since the aunts had reduced our food allowance greatly. We could amass back on the porch or the nearby yard in a flash, the moment the click of an aunt's open toed shoes on the wooden floor of the house sounded anywhere near the front screen door. There we would be sitting, looking repentant and angelic, horn-rimmed glasses hanging on for dear life on the ends of noses, eyes hidden by the glare of the porch light on the thick lenses.

It was during these time-outs that we played one of the games that I now believe shaped our destinies more than anything else. On the east side of our grandmother's house on the lawn before it began its descent to the swampy area below, was a hill of sorts, covered by the greenest, softest, most beautiful grass that grew anywhere on the farm. It was here that we played king of the hill. The object of the game was to gain and keep control of the top of the hill. One could employ any measures necessary to keep everyone else off. This could involve kicking, pushing, hitting, tripping, and yes, even the snatching of someone's glasses, rendering them blind and helpless. There were really no rules, and amazingly, no one was ever hurt. This was all thanks to the cushion of the grass that was so lush it could have been from the Garden of Eden. We rolled down in it, crawled up in it, fell into it, threw it, got hit by clumps of it, swallowed bits of it, and in all truthfulness, wallowed in it like pigs do in mud.

Of course, the largest and strongest cousins were usually the victors as they could easily block or push down the smaller and weaker ones. But, there were times when the weakest cousins joined forces, went on a full-out assault and toppled the reigning king. This didn't happen often as there was always a most unpleasant consequence, usually involving the dethroned king tripping you and pressing down on you with his or her full weight until the lush grass of the hill seemed to fill your mouth and nose. This wasn't about swallowing your pride. For those agonizing minutes you were a cow and eating enough of the lush green grass to sustain you for the winter.

Were our mothers aware of where we were? Of course. There had been so many other times when we weren't in front porch time-out, when it was so hot and humid and the last morsel of food from the kitchen table had been consumed, that they congregated on the porch, the light on so they could see to mash blackheads on another aunt's shoulders or rewind a roller that had somehow loosened, or discuss what was going to happen to their husbands when they returned, that they watched us play our game. Not one, not even our grandmother, ever said anything to stop us. No one said, "Hey, you kids do know where you're playing?" Were they never concerned? After all, this was the same group that admonished us for leaving the house with our hair wet, or warned us not to talk on the phone or stand too close to a window during a thunderstorm. These were the same mothers who prevented us from swimming immediately after eating, demanded we wear coats lest we catch our death of colds and that warned us that someone might commit the worst of all possible acts and hit us on the head.

It wasn't until we were adults that we learned where we had really been playing. The hill was created when they buried the septic tank for our grandmother's house. The grass was green and lush because the seepage from the tank provided the richest of fertilizers, decomposed human waste. It is an eye-opening and somewhat crappy epiphany to learn you had never really played king of the hill. All of those years we had been playing king of the septic tank. We had wallowed on it and in it, until it had permeated every pore of our bodies.

Now that we are grown and looking back with some measure of disbelief at our mothers' judgment, I am not so sure that we did not become stronger because of it. We have assimilated into the world and no longer look like "boat people." Our glasses are more modern, thinner or have been replaced by contacts. We finally gained control of our hair, allowing the ones that still have hair to choose styles that don't come from a third world country. For the most part, we have gained intelligence and sense, though there are a few who remain circumspect. And finally, we are not as easily offended by others as most people are. They can throw it at us, involve us in it, give it to us, or even drag us through it, but it doesn't matter because we grew up immersed in it. Erma Bombeck was correct. The grass does grow greener over the septic tank. We should know. We grew up there.

Fireworks

It is a holiday. Picture a family sitting in lawn chairs or on quilts spread across the lawn. Everyone's eyes are wide open and their hearts are beating at a slightly faster rhythm. They are all anticipating the beauty of the fireworks that will soon start exploding in the night sky. This is not my family. We were rarely passive when fireworks were involved. The only time we were remotely passive was when our father brought home rocket propellant from where he worked. Geez, the security must have been of the highest level at his job. He could have been trading with the Russians for all they knew. Anyway, our dad, the rocket propellant smuggler, constructed rockets with cherry bombs affixed to the tops. The rockets would travel so far into the sky that the exploding cherry bombs were beyond our hearing range.

The danger of the propellant was why my brothers and I were passive. When it came to other fireworks, the sky was the limit, or in our case, the sky really had nothing to do with it.

We were so aggressive with fireworks that it was a miracle none of us were ever hurt. When I ponder where this aggressiveness originated, I can only surmise that most of it came from our mother. Since both our parents were athletic, we were raised to be competitive in just about everything we did. But our mother took it to another extreme. If we were playing badminton, she would rather drive a birdie with full force into the head of an opponent than score a point. If it was croquet, and her ball was positioned where she could hit the pole and win the game, she would choose to tap against an opponent's ball and drive it completely out of the yard. So is it any wonder that we found ways to be both competitive and aggressive when fireworks were available to us?

Now that I think about it, there were only three injuries resulting from shooting fireworks. One of them I will recount later, but the first two had to do with my oldest brother and our dog, Scout. The first injury was to my oldest brother and resulted from a complete disregard for common sense. We were out in the front yard shooting firecrackers. We weren't blowing up anthills or frogs or doing anything remotely destructive. We were never cruel kids. However, we weren't as safe as we should have been. We were lighting firecrackers and throwing them into the air to watch them explode. My middle brother and I had our stashes in piles on the ground. Our oldest brother chose to keep his stash in one of the pockets of the cardigan sweater he was wearing. All was going to plan (just like in a Hallmark movie) until my oldest brother, after lighting and throwing a firecracker, became careless with dropping the match he had just used. Unlike in a Hallmark movie, the match was not completely out, defied reasonable odds and fell into the pocket containing his stash of firecrackers. The next thing we knew he was a whirling dervish, screaming and running in circles. It seemed like every time he ran past us another firecracker would explode. This seemed to go on forever with his screaming to make it stop while he slapped haphazardly at the pocket. We could not have helped him had it been possible, because we were laughing so hard we were on the ground. When the final firecracker exploded, he was able to stop running and assess the damage. The bottom of his sweater pocket was completely gone and gray to black gunpowder marks were streaked on his shirt, pants and hand. If a forensic scientist had been looking for a killer based on firecracker powder residue, my brother would have been in prison. In the end, his wounds were miraculously small. Only minor burns on his hand resulted. The sweater, however, was sent to the morgue.

The second injury occurred to our dog, Scout. Scout was a collie mix. We didn't generally have pure breed dogs. We had the dogs that people gave away. Scout was one of those and a good dog to my brothers and me. Anyway, on this particular day, we had the rare cache of cherry bombs to amuse us. These are a step above firecrackers in value, explosiveness and danger. Their cost meant we only had a few and had to share. Their added explosiveness didn't deter us as we threw them just like firecrackers. We had never witnessed Scout being a fetcher. I think we threw sticks from time to time and he chased them, but I don't remember his ever bringing them back. I think he just liked to run them down and check out what we were throwing. So, on this day we weren't wary as the first cherry bomb was tossed. We weren't even concerned when Scout dashed in the direction it was thrown. It exploded well before Scout even got within range. It was only when the second one was tossed that we experienced any apprehension. It seems Scout was more prepared this time and had we not shrieked like a bunch of banshees for him to come back, he might have gotten too close. So we took turns holding him after that. But just as kids often do, we became lax in our diligence. We may have been down to the last one or at least close. One of us lit the fuse and hurled the bomb as far away as he could. It was like a slow motion movie. We could see the brown fur on Scout's back pushed back by the wind as he darted like a racing dog toward the place the cherry bomb was sailing. Our yells were lost as his strides seem to reach the speed of light. In the end, he was probably no more than a couple of feet away when it exploded. A canine angel must have been looking down as Scout was not mortally wounded. His hearing, on the other hand, was impacted, because for days he didn't respond to our calls. You could be standing right behind him calling him to supper and he wouldn't move. Eventually, his hearing returned, but I don't think he chased anything including sticks after that.

The third injury did not result from an accident. It occurred during one of our favorite things to do with fireworks. We called it bottle rocket battles. There were certain precipitating factors necessary for a true bottle rocket battle to occur. First, our cousins had to be visiting from Michigan and North Carolina. This provided sufficient troops with my brothers and me to properly engage in battle. Second, our fathers had to want a free night so that they could drive around and drink beer as far away from their wives and families as possible. In order to acquire this freedom, they were more than happy to purchase an ample supply of fireworks for their children. The last and probably most important factor was that our mothers had to want a night away from their husbands and kids, so that they could eat at a leisurely pace while pausing to tease each other's hair or mash on a worrisome patch of blackheads. When the planets aligned, so to speak, we were ready to battle.

The battlefield: Our grandmother's house and front yard that sat on the top of a hill. On the east side it sloped down toward a field, swamp and our Uncle Verm's house. On the west side it sloped into our Aunt Dudie's front yard. In both sloping areas there were ditches, grassy mounds where the ground was never leveled and natural sinkholes that just seemed to appear from time to time. All these areas made perfect positions for teams to set up their posts from which to attack. Choosing your spot depended on your intended strategy. For instance, if you planned on any advancing assaults with your bottle rockets, it was best to start on top of the hill. It was difficult to light a rocket and fire it with any accuracy while running uphill. With that said, a position on top of the hill gave you the least amount of coverage from aerial attacks. It also placed you smack dab in the middle of the battlefield with other teams flanking you on both sides. If you wished to remain in camp and launch attacks from only your bottle or pipe, then one of the dips or ditches in the side slopes was your best bet. Actually in the end, I think strategy in choosing was a moot point as usually the oldest cousins always chose the top of the hill with the rest falling in line according to age. In this scheme, my team always seemed to end up behind the smallest hill and closest to the swamp.

The combatants: First, there was my brother Johnny, who was five years older than I, my brother Greg, who was four years older than I, our cousin Twalla, Aunt Dudie and Uncle Ken's only child, who was about my age, and me. In the earlier battles there was also Uncle Verm's daughter Brenda, who was a couple of years older than Johnny. She wasn't there for the later battles because she discovered there were more appropriate social engagements than trying to hit your relatives with firecrackers on sticks. Next were the cousins visiting. Aunt Ruth and Uncle Vernon lived in Georgia for a while and then later in North Carolina. When they came to visit they brought their son Mike, who was about Greg's age and their daughter Pat, whose age was between Greg's and mine.

Mike was rough and tough even back then. If you wanted someone super aggressive on your team, he was the one. Just how tough he actually was, was demonstrated several years later when he was in high school. Though he was hit by a car (he was on foot) on the way to one of his football games, he didn't tell the coach until the game was over. Even that wouldn't have happened had he not collapsed and then had to be rushed to the hospital. It turned out that he had played the entire game with several broken bones and fractures. None of us were ever heralded for good judgment.

Pat was his complete opposite. She was girly and prissy, but had an infectious sense of humor. Her humor made her an ideal teammate in the foxhole, as entertaining conversation serves one well in the midst of battle. She was also good at handing you rockets when you needed them, that was unless she was too busy shrieking after a rocket had landed precariously close to her.

Uncle Verb and Aunt Lucille lived in Kalamazoo, Michigan. Their brood consisted of five daughters. Sherine was the oldest and Johnny's age. Kathy was the next oldest and was Greg's age. Denise, the third daughter was close to Pat's age. Then there was Lynette who was a couple of years younger than Twalla and I. Last, there was Kimmy who was pretty much a toddler at the time. Through some twist of fate, Sherine was the only one of her family that wore glasses. Unlike our run-of-the-mill brown spectacles, hers were pearly white. Kathy had permanent pin curls on either side of her face that were anchored by bobby pins. The bobby pins must have been part of her style as they always seemed to be there like a beauty mark or a tattoo. Denise was long-legged like a grasshopper, which served her well in battle, whether attempting an assault or retreating after her post had been breached. Lynette was a tad young to be a participant. She was a protected observer which meant that any team that had her was responsible for ensuring she wasn't in any danger. This added responsibility handicapped a team in their ability to maneuver in any aggressive manner. Kimmy, of course, had to remain in the house.

The battle: Of the many battles we had, I will recount only one. It was not only the most memorable one, but also the time the third injury occurred. Johnny and Sherine being the oldest, had commandeered the central post at the peak of the hill. Greg and Kathy had established their camp on the western side in front of Aunt Dudie and Uncle Ken's house. Mike and Denise were set up on the eastern slope toward the swamp. Twalla, Pat and I were relegated to what was left, a small ditch-like position, somewhere between Aunt Dudie's and Grandma's yards. As the battle began, no one was truly in danger. Rockets were fired from a wide assortment of coke bottles. Please note that by coke bottles I don't necessarily mean Coca Cola bottles. They

were most probably Dr. Pepper, Pepsi, Mountain Dew and some Coca
Cola bottles. However, we called them all cokes. Our northern cousins
always found that amusing as they called them all pop. Regardless of
the brand, they were the launchers for each camp.

Trajectory was managed using rocks, small limbs or for the truly
lucky, a short piece of a two by four. In the early goings, we were
constantly changing the position of the bottle against the prop to get our
rockets as close as possible to the camp or camps we were assaulting.
What this meant for us who had poor eyesight, battling in yards barely
bathed in moonlight with the absence of porch lights and the lack of
common sense and good judgment, was that there were a whole lot
of bottle rockets that were simply shot in crazy arches toward no one
in particular and that landed in bushes, trees or on the gravel road. As
the battle progressed, however, our trajectories became more accurate
and the occasional ending "pops" of the exploding rockets would elicit
yelps from the camps where they had landed too close for comfort.

Yelps were, of course, supposed to be stifled so your position was
not compromised, and also to deprive the other teams the pleasure of
knowing they had almost gotten you. Pat, one of my teammates, was
never good at stifling her yelps. Quite the opposite was true for her. Her
yelps were piercing, much like a wild animal caught in a trap. Since we
were the youngest team in the battle, we were also the favorite target.
It was as if the other teams had developed an extremely strong sense
of hearing to compensate for poor eyesight. Like bats, they honed in
closer and closer to our position each time Pat shrieked.

We would have probably been the first team doomed to defeat had it
not been for Cousin Mike's restless aggressive nature that was hankering
for some real action. Out of the darkness he charged the hill holding a
lighted Roman candle and firing the colorful fireballs toward Johnny
and Sherine's camp. It was a crazy, devilish and almost successful plan
had the Roman candle not sputtered out within yards of their position.
It then became a foolish strategic blunder as all camps turned their
full rocket fire on Mike as he fled across the yard. He wasn't hit, but

you could see the outline of his body as rockets whistled all around him, with a few exploding so close that I'm sure he lost his hearing advantage for the rest of the battle.

It was shortly after this ill-fated assault that the third fireworks-related injury occurred. For some unknown reason, though we all guessed it involved food, our Aunt Lucille decided to saunter from our grandmother's house down to Aunt Dudie's. There was no such thing as a ceasefire in our battles. So, the minute she stepped off Grandma's porch she was walking into an active war zone. She seemed to have safely achieved her goal as she ascended the steps to Dudie's house when out of nowhere, it seemed, a rocket streaked through the night sky and struck with a crazy thudding sound into her right thigh. Lucky for her, it didn't explode until it dropped to the porch. Unlucky for us, her yell ended with the porch lights of both houses turning on and a covey of aunts, forks still in their hands from grazing, issuing strong warnings and admonitions about shooting rockets toward the houses. It seems they were chuckling under their breaths about Aunt Lucille's injury, but felt the need to chastise us, and in so doing, unruffle Aunt Lucille's ruffled feathers. Luckily for her and us, her only resulting injury was a small bruise.

So, the battle began again with one major change. The porch lights remained on. Unfortunately for Johnny and Sherine, Grandma's porch light spotlighted the exact location of their camp. So, all camps began an all-out assault on their position. It was just a matter of time before someone's rocket struck pay dirt. Even though all laid claim to the masterful shot that brought about their demise, in the end it was probably just a fluke. Anyway, someone's bottle rocket arched into the dark farm sky and then dropped directly into the middle of their cache of rockets. When it exploded, it set off a chain of reactions. Bottle rockets from their cache began firing in all directions. Sherine and Johnny had no other recourse but to roll as quickly as they could in opposite directions from their camp. Had they stood, they no doubt would have been hurt. For what seemed to be an interminable length of time, their camp looked like a fountain with rockets firing in cascades in Grandma's yard. Amidst the sounds of the exploding rockets you could hear all the members of the other teams laughing unmercifully, and mixed in were the occasional shrieks of horror from Johnny and Sherine as they rolled and rolled and rolled until the last rocket fired. There wasn't much reason to continue to battle after that. We weren't ones to gloat for very long. We preferred good natured laughter. So, after we had laughed so hard that some unnamed cousins almost peed on themselves, and we had helped Johnny and Sherine brush away the grass and various other things that stuck to them during their Olympic-worthy rolls, we were ready to move on. Even though there were rockets left, the battle was over. There was still time for a game of kick-the-can.

Firework displays are now grandiose. Sweeping cascades of colors and sparkling explosions fill the sky. Families sit back and marvel at the magnificence of the displays. When the show is over, they gather their blankets, chairs, trash and children and head back to the sanctity of their homes. What they don't take with them is what we experienced all those years ago. The fireworks were much simpler. But, when we interacted with them they fed our imaginations. We became soldiers and mad scientists. We had secret powers with the lighting of tiny fuses. We were human fireflies that raced through the night. We didn't watch a show. We were the show.

On some nights, if I try really hard, I can see bottle rockets cross the sky. I can hear firecrackers popping, cherry bombs exploding and Scout barking. And even though Johnny and Mike are no longer with us, they still appear. I see Johnny wearing the cardigan with a pocket missing, and Mike reckless and laughing, charging the hill with a Roman candle. We are all still young, carrying bundles of bottle rockets to our posts. We are at our grandmother's farm where all is good. The night belongs to the cousins and we still have the sparkle of fireworks in our eyes.

Walks With Grandma

Water can be peaceful and almost hypnotic when it blocks or muffles the sounds of the world. It can lull you and make you melancholic when it is moving in a leisurely fashion over rocks in small streams and creeks. It can conjure images in your head of things lost or things to be found as it moves slowly but assuredly in long ribbons of rivers. It can become one with your heartbeat as an ocean with its waves pulsing against the shores. It can also be powerful and angry. It must have been very angry on that day when its river's course that it had followed forever was blocked by a dam. What ensued was an untamed fury when it was forced to retreat. For compensation it claimed innumerable small valleys and fields. It took the house where my grandmother was raised. It took the land where her father who was of Native American descent hunted, trapped and fished to provide for her family. It wiped away any evidence of that part of her life just as her mother's crude broom swept away all footprints from the dirt floor at the end of a day.

I wonder now if that was what was going through her mind when she paused during one of our walks. She would become very still and close her eyes. Other than the slight fluttering of her eyelids there was no discernible movement. Was she hearing the roar of the river as it swept away all that was part of her childhood? Were there visions of her parents and siblings and ancestors as she knew them during her early years suspended in water? She never spoke to me of it. She would sigh as if expelling water from her lungs, smile at me and once again start walking.

There were many things about her including her childhood I didn't know at the time and some things I had heard, and whether true or not, discounted. It is the way we see people that we love with our whole hearts I know now. She was by no means perfect. But with love we tend to see more with our hearts than our heads. All the bad things become peripheral, faint and almost obscure. That is the way I saw her. I have found the opposite to be true when looking at someone we don't like. The bad things about them seem to become magnified and overwhelming while the good things dart about waiting for us to grab hold of them. That was the way I was with my grandfather. I wish I had made more of an attempt to reach for the good things. But I didn't and as a result never really knew him.

When Grandma and I walked we always followed the same initial path. Since her house was nestled on top of the hill, we began on a descent through her backyard, past the cottonwood tree where my cousins and I had climbed and hid and lost ourselves in countless fantasy worlds, past the old well house that still carried a rich damp smell though it was no longer in use, past the barn and shed that still housed some outdated and no longer functional equipment and where her grandchildren had fought hundreds of wars with corncobs and rocks and then to the beginning of the back fields farm road at the far edge of the yard. When we reached this point, her smile always broadened. Her feet seemed to rise a little higher off the ground. I think she was already thinking of the things she wanted to share with me. It was a moment in time when possibilities outweighed expectations and when what could be came wrapped like a present.

She was still agile at the time, surprising since she had given birth to eight children all at home and without assistance, or so I've been told. Grandpa always seemed to be away when she was in labor. It sounds callous and neglectful, but in truth he worked in many capacities to support the family. He was a farmer, land surveyor, unschooled veterinarian, music teacher and gospel singer. This is not to say Grandma was totally okay with his constant absence. On at least one occasion that I'm aware of, it came to a head. It was the singing gigs that got her. Regardless of the fact he was singing gospel songs, I think in her mind this offered the opportunity for philandering. So, one day she snapped. She told him he wasn't going. He said he was. She, who didn't know how to drive, marched out the front door, got in his car, started it and then literally drove it up a tree. When she came back in the house, she told him to go if he must, but he'd be walking.

It was this tenacious and resilient woman that stood next to me at the bottom of the yard and the beginning of the farm road. Maybe, the image of the car astride the thick trunk of the holly tree is what crossed her mind as we continued on our walk. She had a way of taking in a quick gulp of air at the same time that she touched her tongue to the roof of her mouth that made her false teeth emit a clicking sound. Over the years I came to equate this sound with either her discontent with something or someone, or either her sheer joy at what was happening. At that juncture of yard and road on this day, she offered a series of these clicks almost as if she was about to break into a Flamingo dance. She couldn't drive, but she could on occasion dance with the devil.

From this point the farm road continued down the first terrace toward a wet weather creek. I don't know if the terraces on the land were natural with the way the land lay or created with the growing of a variety of crops and the necessity of draining those areas. But we had made our way down the first terrace to where the persimmon tree grew. Grandma would first eye the persimmons for color and then hold one in her hand to check for firmness. There would be a click or two as she went through this process. If they were ripe, she would nod her head to give me the go-ahead while popping the persimmon in her mouth. I could see the orange juice squeeze out between her lips and run down her chin. I was never fond of the flavor. It seemed too earthy for me. But I would eat them when I was with her. It was another eye-closing time for her. I think she remembered times with her siblings when sugar wasn't abundant and they had to rely on nature's sweeteners. It must have been ecstasy for them. I could see that same feeling on her face at that moment. Then there would be a click and a laugh as she reminded me I didn't want to ever put an unripe persimmon in my mouth. There was no need for the warning. Growing up with a slew of cousins and a grandfather who thrived on pranks, I had experienced the unpleasantness of the horrendously tart flavor more than once. They should use them instead of Botox treatments. The extreme puckering of your lips removes every line from your face.

A series of terraces led us to higher ground. Each terrace prompted a recounting of the crops that were raised there. Most years it was cotton and she reminded me, as if my mother had not, that her children spent many days hoeing around the cotton plants to rid them of the ever-encroaching weeds. And then it was watching the weather. The rain was something they couldn't control. Too much and the plants would rot; too little and they would wilt. So, there must have been days when she stood at her kitchen window and surveyed the fields for glimpses of her children working or looked for signs to read regarding the weather. This perpetual waiting game had creased her face and age was making her skin papery thin. As she talked she'd reach up a hand to block the sun while pivoting her head to do a slow scan. I would hear a slower and more languid click. I thought at that moment she might have transported herself back in time and into her kitchen. But, before I could ask, she would talk of the whiteness that all of a sudden came one day and spread across the land like a freshly laundered sheet. Her kids, she told me, would trade in their hoes for sacks. They would pick from sunrise till sunset. She would sometimes have to doctor their hands in the evenings to soothe the cuts and scratches from the sharp edges of the cotton bolls. Strange, she would intone as she turned to begin walking again, how something so wonderfully soft could come from a husk so hard with pointy barbs. She would get ahead of me a pace as I was transfixed, still looking for the white. And I thought of her kids. Maybe, she was thinking of them as she spoke. My aunts and uncles and mother had a softness in them too, but also a protective husk that could slice you if you weren't careful. My brothers, cousins and I have the scars to prove it.

When I realized she had walked on, I would race to catch up to her. It was the only time that I felt compelled to move with any speed. There was a contentment just being with her. It was a time and place you didn't want to hurry through for fear of missing something. We could have been figures in a snow globe with the only music the clicking of her teeth. She had not gone far, only one terrace up. From there, looking back, you could see the grove of trees that produced the small red apples she used to make her fried pies. She looked in that direction and smiled. I couldn't help but smile too. Being one of her favorites, she hid pies for me and another select few as well. However, it was an almost wicked game she played. For her grandchildren she wasn't partial to, she'd often claim the pies were all gone while winking at the rest of us. It was if we were in a James Bond movie and our grandmother was Goldfinger. Her kitchen was Fort Knox and the fried apple pies were the gold bullion. As soon as the grandchildren that posed a threat to national kitchen security left, she would produce pies from some secret alcove of one of her cabinets, set them on the table, and while clicking the James Bond theme song with her teeth, go for the butter to smear on top of them.

It was a short walk from there to the edge of the woods. The woods were sprawling and covered hills, dips and ravines. They led eventually to overgrown fields that had once grown crops and finally a creek where my brothers, cousins and I had spent many days catching crawdads with our forked sticks or gathering scaly barks when the time was right. Though she was able to move easily, we wouldn't venture far into the woods. It seemed enough for her to be able to enter the edge of them. What was beyond was already firmly ensconced in her memory. So, we looked for the muscadine vines to see if they would bear a hearty crop that year. If we were lucky, they were in season and she could once again school me on how to tell when they were just right for eating. We'd pick them one by one, squeezing their hard casings to force the inner fruit to pop into our mouths. It was a sweetness that made us both smile and even laugh had our mouths not been fighting to hold it all in. Her teeth seemed to click after each one she ate. And she would speak of the jelly she could make with them. And a pretty good wine, she would add, as she winked at me like I was her partner in a dubious business venture. When we'd had our fill, muscadine casings littered the ground around us like casualties from a war. They had met their match in my grandmother and me.

To counter any trace of the purple color that might taint our lips or teeth, we always visited the sweet gum tree. It was my grandmother's favorite. As a child, she told me, they didn't have toothbrushes, or as she described them, any other fancy things to clean their teeth with. They had always used twigs of the sweet gum to rub across their teeth to remove stains and clean them. And the sweet flavor would freshen their breath. So, she would break off two twigs and pull apart the ends to form bristles. As she handed me mine, she would remind me to not only swab my teeth, but to also suck in the juice and savor the sweetness. There we'd stand with our sweet gum toothbrushes in our mouths, swabbing and sucking and both lost in two different worlds. For her I think the sweet gum took her to all the places she'd been in her life and evoked images of the people she'd encountered along the way. For me, it simply took me to her. The taste of the sweet gum was the flavor of my grandmother. It was the flavor of contentment.

We didn't pause as often when we turned and headed back to her house. We moved at a slower pace. It wasn't because we were tired, but that we were carrying more thoughts and feelings than when we came. There were sounds and visions and tastes and words and memories that traveled back with us. It was as if we had claimed a piece of important luggage to bring home. You could feel the weight of it, but at the same time its content was so dear that the extra burden was as welcome as a long lost friend returning home. Terrace to terrace we walked, over the field where you could see the apple tree grove, across the field where brown gave way to green and then exploded into white when the cotton was ready for picking, over the wet weather creek where the sweet earthy scent of the persimmon tree lingered, and then up the terraces to the farmhouse where my grandmother and I would rest and catch our breath in the swing on her front porch. There weren't many words exchanged then, only her occasional clicks and from me deep breaths followed by long languid sighs as if all that was important in life had entered my lungs and then needed to escape.

It has been many years since my grandmother died. And since then I have become a much more impatient person. When driving, I am possessed by a demon and spout incredibly foul epithets toward other drivers who interfere with the speed I try to maintain in reaching my destination. In stores, I wish other shoppers that do not move with the same quick clip as me to dematerialize or transport to another dimension. I am caught up or perhaps possessed by my destinations and purposes rather than the journeys to get there. In so doing, I am missing all the things you find along the way, good and bad, that my grandmother taught me to be mindful of and appreciate the importance of.

I need to return to her farm and retrace our steps. On those terraces and in those woods I know she waits for me. All I have to do is walk slowly, pausing at times to take in everything around me. Maybe, she will come when I see the apple trees once more, or close my eyes and imagine myself between rows of robust and green cotton plants with their bolls almost at the point of opening and spewing forth the soft whiteness, or when I fray the end of a twig from a sweet gum tree and with the swab of my teeth savor the sweetness that fills my mouth. She will be there, I know, if I take the time, All I have to do is be still and listen. As if from nowhere she will come, the sound of her quick intake of breath at the same time she touches her tongue to the roof of her mouth, and the discordant click that resonates within me. She is always a click away.

Slide Shows

My father was a dutiful chronicler of our lives in pictures. He
started at a time when slides were the thing. We had the small
hand-held devices that showed one slide at a time, then a projector that
was fed by a box of slides, and finally one that would operate using
carousels. At first a screen was used to display the images, and later a
blank wall seemed to do the trick just as well. There were slide shows
anytime relatives or friends came to visit. We'd fill the couches, chairs
and floor in anticipation of the nostalgic moments when the images
would take us back to trips or gatherings, or to people that were no
longer with us. Most of us were apprehensive because there were always
one or two slides (and for some even more) that caught us either at our
worst or seemed to exaggerate things about us that made us insecure.

The odds of either of these being caught in a picture were huge as we were truly not an attractive lot. It served you well if you controlled the projector. You could speed through the pictures of yourself while pausing the laughter-provoking ones of your brothers and cousins for deliciously long lengths of times.

Since Daddy was almost always the photographer, Mother, my brothers and I were in many of the pictures captured. There she was to the side, with my brothers and me posing around another state sign. My dad seemed obsessed with this particular backdrop, and my brothers and I were willing stooges, forming letters with our hands to match those on the signs, sprawled across the tops of them, or acting as if we were representatives of the state we were entering with our arms spread wide to welcome all that came after us. We probably had the opposite effect and were the unidentified factor that caused significant drops in tourism the years we were there. There was one slide with Mother's face through the windshield of our Dodge Dart when she refused to get out of the car as the ferry boat took us across the Mississippi River. My brothers and I are pictured leaning precariously over the railing of the ferry obviously entranced by the muddy waters below. We had to be entranced. At the slightest sign of discontent, we were lectured on how we didn't know how lucky we were, as in this case to be crossing a river.

The bottom line was, we didn't travel a lot and when we did the destination had to be where relatives lived. That was the only way it fit into the family budget and on those trips the budget did not allow for many stops, state signs excluded. In fact, we only stopped when the car needed refueling. Otherwise, we were in the car for the long haul which could be up to ten or twelve hours. Mother had packed sandwiches, snacks and drinks to sustain us for the trip. My brothers and I had pillows to sleep on in the back seat. Being the youngest and smallest, I was always relegated to either the floorboard or the back window. In the back window I was smashed into an unnatural position against the glass. In the floorboard, I had to contend with the hump in the middle or the housing for the axle of the car. I should have been wearing a tee shirt that said, "Future Chiropractor's Dream."

If that were not enough, we were allowed no bathroom stops unless they coincided with the refueling of the car. If one of my brothers or I became desperate, our mother would pass an empty Dr. Pepper bottle over the seat to us. Dr. Pepper was our cola of choice and we were allotted one case per month. My brothers and I could decide how often and when we drank them. Most of the time they were gone in a week or two which meant we did without for the rest of the month. They were too extravagant and outside the budget for our trips. Kool-Aid mixed in a gallon jug was what we were offered, and again complaints were not an option. Anyway, we'd take the Dr. Pepper bottle, pee in it, pass it back to her and she would hold the container of warm urine until there came a time our dad had to slow down or stop at a sign or light. Then she would quickly roll down her window and pour it out. The empty bottle would be stored in the floorboard for future recycling necessities. It would have made for a wonderful Dr. Pepper commercial, something like we put the "P" back in Pepper. Of course, it could have only been shown on TV in some Scandinavian country.

During the slide shows, the ones of our family trips were moved through quickly unless they included other family members present. This was a great relief to my brothers and me as some of the most embarrassing ones were of us. We didn't escape from all of them however. Our cousins, aunts and uncles were too savvy to allow that to happen. When a particularly embarrassing slide from one of our trips or just our daily life appeared, my brothers and I would become suddenly quiet and attempt to melt into the throng, while willing our dad to change to the next slide. Someone, usually a cousin, would yell, "Wait! Oh my gosh, is that you? What were you thinking?" For what seemed an eternity, projected on the wall was my oldest brother wearing the most unattractive glasses and manning an artillery gun on the USS Wilmington. It was as if our nation was at war and in such dire need of servicemen that even my brother, though only fourteen, had been conscripted. "What are your qualifications, son?" To which my brother replied in a shaky voice, " I'm learning to play the tenor sax, sir." "Perfect. You're just right to man an artillery gun on a warship."

Or there was the one of my middle brother wearing his junior high school basketball uniform and his thick horn-rimmed glasses. He is posed on the front porch of our house. He has one knee crooked and a basketball held above his head like he is about to shoot at some imaginary goal in the middle of our front yard. He is so skinny that the uniform he is wearing looks like it really belongs to a much bigger player that has graciously offered it up to my brother for this once-in-a-lifetime photo op. Someone with a discerning eye could have pegged him as a Ukrainian exchange student that had been raised on one bowl of turnips a day. Then there were his socks. Mother had to have modified them in some way, either adding elastic or taking out a one inch strip for them to hold on to his ankles that were so small they resembled the dowels that hold towels in the bathroom. I can imagine my dad prepping him for the shot. "There are three seconds left on the clock. You have the last shot. The goal is by the holly bush next to the sidewalk. Shoot," and an infamous picture was born.

As for me, there were so many that made me cringe, but one particular one taken when I was older and out of college still haunts me. It is a picture of Mother and me. Since the hair on the top of my head had receded and left only a wispy point, I had grown out the sides and back to compensate. I had also grown the strangest sideburns that wove under the sides of my chin. Why no one told me that I had chosen a most unbecoming style baffles me still. In the picture I am wearing a tux that was rented for the wedding of two of my African American friends that I worked with. It was an elaborate affair in one of Macon, Georgia's largest Catholic churches. I was the only Caucasian member of the wedding party. The only really tense moment occurred when at rehearsal the pairings of groomsmen and bridesmaids was set. The bridesmaid assigned for me to escort had a momentary flash of horror cross her face. I thought I was experiencing what discrimination felt like. But, with the hairdo and sideburns I was sporting, I'm guessing she wasn't focused as much on the fact that I was white as my overall appearance. "Does he speak English," she must have thought. "Does he work in a circus sideshow? Do they know he's missing from the asylum?" In the end, all went well except I could feel that she only held my arm by the very tips of her fingers, and I'm not sure, but I think I detected the bulk of an additional set of gloves.

It was Mother's idea for the picture. She had donned a floor length black and white flowery dress that we didn't even know she had, and stood with her arm woven in mine as if I were her escort. We are posed in front of our house like she is my prom date and our parents want some quick shots. That is a scary idea in itself. We look like we are actors from the TV show, *Dark Shadows*. I could have been Barnabas Collins's son, or at least his hapless and naive victim. The hapless and naive part certainly was plausible. My grandmother would have found confirmation when I told her, "You were right. I was out last night after eight o'clock. I didn't get hit on the head, but I did get bitten by a vampire." Neither my mother nor I are smiling in the picture. If we had been, I'm sure you would have been able to see our fangs, unless it was shot from a reflection in a mirror. Then you wouldn't have seen us at all.

My brothers and I weren't always in the safe zone even when the pictures were of other members of the family. Unfortunately, we were in many of those as well. But, we had the advantage of having been in on every slide show and as a result knew them so well that we were ready to deflect attention to someone else in the picture. A slide taken in Okefenokee Swamp Park is a good case in point. We were visiting our Aunt Ruth and Uncle Vernon in Brunswick, Georgia. The day trip to the park was an added treat. The picture in question is taken in front of a sign proclaiming that scenes from the movie, "Swamp Water," had been filmed there. Hello, sign, movie. It's a miracle that the picture isn't fuzzy from my dad's hands shaking from the sheer excitement of it all. There are my brothers, our cousin Mike and me in squatted positions and resembling much of the wildlife in the park. Really, a gator should have risen up and taken at least one of us into the swamp for his family to nibble on. "Look, honey, nuggets for the kids." In the back stands our mother in a stylish full-skirted dress that was perfectly suited for a swamp tour. She is holding a black purse that appears large enough to carry a couple of empty Dr. Pepper bottles. You just never know with three boys. Beside her is her niece who wants to be just like her, our cousin Pat. Pat looks like a female version of my brothers, our cousin Mike and me. She is wearing horn-rimmed glasses and a shorts outfit like the rest of us. She always complained of being overweight, however in her defense the rest of us were so darned skinny we looked malnourished. So she always appeared bigger. Our grandmother would have called her healthy-looking or big-boned. One thing that allowed us to deflect to her in the picture was the large purse she carried to mimic our mother. I mean what all did she have to carry? She was ten years old, for gosh sake. However, her real downfall was the Brownie camera she wore around her neck. Unfortunately for her, we all knew she never had film for it. I guess she thought it made her look more adult-like or maybe she viewed it as a fashion accessory, which might have worked if we had been mingling with the crowds in the streets of Rome. So when the slide popped up, before anyone could comment on the gator bait squatting on the ramp, one of my brothers or I would quickly question, "What's that around Pat's neck?"

There were a group of slides of the family taken at a Summer reunion at Guntersville Lake. These always elicited a gamut of emotions. One minute everyone would be laughing so hard that the bathroom became the equivalent of a porta potty at a concert. Suddenly there would be a strange silence when the adults in particular were lost in their memories. They were the keepers of the back stories for the pictures on the wall. Each one held something poignant or momentous that led them to reflect on times or places or people. There were the faces of people no longer with us that stared directly at us as if saying, "We are still here."

It was the last time our mother's family was all together. The only one missing was our cousin Dickie. He was the only son of Mother's sister, Sybil. The last time we saw him, he was in his late teens. After that we only heard news of him from Aunt Sybil. He had grown up in Missouri, attended college there and joined the army. The last tidbit we heard before his mother died was that he was an officer stationed in one of the missile silos in the Midwest. He never made contact with anyone in the family, not even our grandmother before she died. Maybe he considered us all a security risk. If you look at us in those pictures, any one of us could have come from one of the cold war countries. Even if the infiltrator had slipped and called our grandmother babushka, we would have been too busy adjusting our glasses or racing in and out of the lake to have noticed.

There is a slide of Grandpa and Grandma with their seven kids standing in a line according to their chronological age. There had been eight, but their daughter Theora had died of colitis at an early age. They all wore broad smiles because the day was one of immense mirth, loud voices, children darting haphazardly in all directions and even some chicanery. We had learned to expect the trickery from our grandpa, but this time it was our grandmother that was the culprit. There is a slide to document the beginning of her actions. It shows her innocently cutting up a watermelon to serve. However, instead of passing one of the slices, she threw it at her youngest daughter catching her fully on the back. What ensued was a watermelon battle of epic proportions. There are no slides of the battle as I'm sure my dad was too busy ducking the rinds, seeds and pieces of melon to snap any. Cleanup was easy since we were eating on the ground and most of the melon was left for the critters in the woods around us. As for the participants in the fight, the lake would take away the sticky residue on our skin and swimsuits.

There is also a slide of all the grandchildren (except Dickie) and even the first great grandchild. What a crew we were in our swimsuits with our genetically-engineered Henson legs that were skinny with knobby knees. The older male cousins had already lost most of their hair. The female cousins were not yet aware that a mutual fate of thinning hair awaited them as they grew older. I am turned sideways with a belly protruding so far out it appears I have swallowed the one watermelon that survived the fight. The top of cousin Pat's swimsuit has dropped to her waist. Luckily, she hadn't gone through puberty yet. It is easy to see to which of the Henson siblings we each belong. Even though we have characteristics inherited from our other parents, on this day and in this picture it is the Henson blood that seems to dominate.

Other slides from that day catch us either sitting or playing in the muddy water of the lake. Where was that flesh-eating bacteria? I don't know if the lake was that color when we arrived or we made it so with our thrashing, swimming or the many water games we played. Our father clicks the projector and there on the wall is my cousin Twalla and me sitting in the water's edge with mud heaped to cover our legs. Beside us are our cousins from Michigan wearing life jackets. I always question when this slide appears, why Twalla and I aren't wearing any flotation devices. Uncle Verb, the Michigan cousins' dad, had brought his ski boat down with him from Kalamazoo. The adults all concur that his daughters must have just gotten off a boat ride. Another interjects that Twalla and I were already good swimmers and didn't need life jackets. Still, I wonder if there wasn't a culling going on, like a survival of the fittest thing. After all there were some huge catfish in that lake. We may not have been the meatiest of meals, but there is no doubt in my mind that we Hensons would be spicy and gamy morsels. "What's that strange and unusual flavor I'm sensing?" one catfish might offer. "Gotta be a Henson," the other would reply.

After Grandmother died, there were no more Henson reunions. Only in the slides can you find them now. The same happened in my family when my dad passed. It is as if some people are the center of things and when the center is gone there is no gravitational pull for everyone else. The last slide shows I can remember only involved my immediate family. In those the focus was more on my nieces and nephews while they were growing up. When the older slides appeared, they would laugh and comment on my brothers, my parents and me and the cousins they knew. But, there were so many faces and people they had never met nor felt any connection to, it was difficult to explain who belonged to whom, and they seemed to lose interest as we tried to recount the back stories to each slide as it appeared on the wall.

It is all a lost art now as people record their pictures on their smart phones and store them in digital albums. They can share them with you or others by passing the phone around for quick glances. It is not the same as those slide shows. There is something about the family as a collective viewing their history projected on a wall or screen. It is a shared consciousness with everyone's memories necessary to make the picture come to life again. What one doesn't remember, someone else does, and even the cacophony of laughs or sighs or even laments from all those viewing the slides are now part of the memories from the shows themselves. When my nieces and nephews saw the slide of Grandma bending to cut the melon what was pictured is all they saw. For those of us that were there, we see a watermelon melee. We see all the people who are no longer here. We hear voices that can't be replicated. The slides are like pieces of a thousand piece puzzle. When they are put together they become a mosaic of who we were, who we are and how the two came together.

The lights dim. The slide projector hums as it warms up. There is a clicking sound. An image appears on the wall. It is a time and place. It is the saga of a family and those that know the back stories will soon be gone.

Home Free

When the moon wasn't full or was covered by clouds, a thick syrupy darkness came with nightfall. The only light came from the porch light or lamps in the windows and even those rectangular protrusions of light didn't reach very far into the yard surrounding the house. They pushed against the dark as best they could, but in the end they seemed more like back-lit portraits in a gallery. The porch light fared better by at least illuminating a small area in front of it and in that small area there was a glint from an object that seemed discordantly placed, a tin can, the Holy Grail of our childhood, patiently waiting for someone's foot to make contact, propelling it into the darkness and starting our games of Kick the Can.

On those most magical nights when the cousins were all gathered and we saw the can sail through the air, we didn't wait to find out where it landed. We scattered in wild dashes to favorite hiding spots. We rolled into ditches and darted under hedges. We crouched behind the old well house and turned sideways to disappear behind the trunks of trees. We lay flat on our stomachs on the ground behind grassy mounds and remained motionless and quiet for as long as we could stand it, waiting for just the right moment to dart to a new hiding spot or throw caution to the wind and run full-out toward the can. We heard the muffled sounds of other cousins hiding near us and wondered if they were also aware of where we were. There was the sound of crickets and the low deep-throat sounds of the bullfrogs in the distant swamp. We watched fireflies fly over and around us. It was as if they were the stars from the night sky above us and had descended to play the game. If there was a breeze, we smelled honeysuckle, jasmine and other sweet aromas from the flowers that Grandma planted and tended in the beds in front of her house. We were wary around the cottonwood tree because the crunching of its dry husks under our feet would give away our position. And always there was the possibility in the backs of our minds, the wonderful almost delectable possibility that we would get the chance to engage in the breathless, no-holds-barred race with the one who was "it" and get there one second before him/her, kick the can farther than it had ever been kicked while yelling with all the breath that was left in us, "Home free!"

For what seemed like forever we nestled, hid, waited and listened as the cousin that was "it" called out the name and position of another cousin. The sound of racing feet ensued as the two dashed to be the first to reach the can. A triumphant cry from "it" pierced the quiet along with a loud sigh from the cousin captured. We shifted positions as one after another were spotted and sent to the porch as "it" yelled their names and positions while setting his or her foot on the top of the can to seal their fate. When there were only a few of us left in the game, we heard the prisoners yelling encouragement. Occasionally they announced "its" position or the direction he or she was going.

We responded accordingly by shifting to new hiding spots opposite that direction. Even then, some were spotted and captured.

In the end, if you were lucky on that night, you were the only one left and the fate of the rest fell heavily on your shoulders. You started thinking about how you could make it to the holly tree. It was a great spot with the can in full view and only a quick dash away. You crawled on your belly until you were in a shallow ditch that was a few yards from the holly. You ceased breathing as the sound of "its" footsteps seemed to be getting closer and closer. When you heard the steps move away from you, your head raised just enough to see that "it" was at the other side of the yard. Before you could think, you were on your feet and darting to hug the back of the trunk of the holly and at the same time willing your breath to be shallow at best. As "it" peered around the far side of the house, you knew it was your chance. You rounded the holly and raced with what seemed a superhuman speed toward the can. "It" was almost too far away to counter, but was the fastest cousin and had everything to lose. The two of you were a blur with the can vivid and almost shining in the porch light. It was a mere fraction of a second that was the difference. As "its" foot was descending on the can, you stretched your leg out as if it were made of rubber and kicked the can as hard as you could. When you yelled, "Home free," it was drowned out by the shrieks of the captured cousins bolting for freedom from the porch and scattering like leaves in a gust of wind.

We were in our forties the last time we played Kick the Can. Our oldest aunt had died and the cousins had congregated at our grand-mother's house in the afternoon after the funeral. As we sat on the porch, we reminisced about our aunt who had been a seamstress who had not only altered hundreds of garments for the patrons at the store where she worked for thirty years, but had also gifted the lucky ones of us with a quilt or one of her wonderfully eccentric homemade sock monkeys. We talked of the child our aunt lost when the horse drawn wagon she and her family were riding in had overturned in a creek that was swollen from days of torrential rains. We spoke of her life like it was a story we had read, a tale filled with an inordinate amount of sadness. Yet, she always seemed to fight for the happy endings and as a result did find at the end of her life some years of reprieve when she was able to be truly carefree and do what she enjoyed most which was to travel. We concluded that we were not as stalwart as she was. Though we had experienced a mere fraction of the obstacles and sadness she had faced and were only half her age, we were already looking forward to when we might find the same reprieve.

As we rehashed stories about her and of growing up together, daylight began to wane and nighttime seemed to settle around us with an ease that only seems to come when you are in the company of old friends. It was perhaps because of that ease along with the nostalgia that had begun to dominate our thinking that the oldest of the cousins who was there suggested we play the game we had relished as kids. It was something we all seemed to need. We needed giddiness to replace the pall. For just a bit, we needed to be kids again.

As one of the cousins set the tin can on the walkway to the porch, the same place it had been in all of our games as kids, we could see there were many things that were different. First of all, the terrain was not the same. The line of huge shrubs on the west side of the house was gone. Many of the smaller bushes in the front yard were also missing. What we had once construed to be ditches were now no more than slight dips in the ground, and the hills we had once fiercely fought to defend were no more than mounds. The flower beds our grandmother had tended with an almost religious fervor no longer existed. The rock and brick outlines that remained were the only things to remind us of where they had been.

If that were not enough, there was no longer a thick and syrupy darkness that facilitated stealth-like assaults on an unguarded can. Houses that had been built in what once was a vacant field across the road had the new motion-controlled outdoor lights that pierced the night at the slightest movement. With these lights there would be no surprise attacks. Any perpetrators would be like deer caught in the headlights of a car, easily identified with their name and location called out by whoever was "it" as he or she touched a foot to the top of the can, and then sent to the porch until someone could free them.

No doubt the most notable difference was in us. The thirty some odd years that had passed since we last played had taken its toll. We carried not only the additional weight we had gained, but also all the things in life, good and bad, that now caused our shoulders to slump. Bad knees, arthritis, and even poorer eyesight would restrict our movements. Maybe the added light in the yard was really a blessing. It would at least keep someone from tripping and getting hurt. We didn't need a broken hip, or any bones for that matter, and certainly not the all-knowing and smug declaration from one of the remaining aunts, "What the heck were you thinking?"

So the game began after much dickering, as if we were still kids, about who would be "it," a truly daunting and thankless position when playing with a bevy of cousins. However, this time it wasn't as contentious since the yard was better lighted and the players much slower. Our oldest cousin conceded to take the job and took her position near the can. The cousin who readily professed to be the best kicker stepped up and assumed a stance as if he were a placekicker on a football team. He took three quick steps and then launched the can into the air and far enough that it left the lighted area of the yard. The distance the can traveled, along with the fact that the cousin who was "it" suffered from the same physical maladies, was enough to give us time to scatter around the house and find hiding places. We may not have been as fast as we were as kids, but we were every bit as loud. There were shrieks and laughter mixed in with the heaving, gasps for breath, moans and creaking of seldom used joints as we disappeared into the darkness.

There weren't many good places to hide anymore. Even though we had tapped into the ten- or eleven-year-old kids we used to be, the increased girth and taller frames of our adult selves made many of the remaining old favorite spots out of the question. A shallow ditch wouldn't come close to hiding a derriere that resembled a fifty-pound bag of potatoes. It was difficult to shrink a six-foot frame to disappear behind a two-foot bush. And if it required squeezing under or through something to reach a safe haven, we were totally out of luck. Even if we had been able at our age to achieve a body re-positioning necessary to get into those tight prized spots, it was doubtful that we would have been able to extricate ourselves from them without the use of a winch or even worse, calling an emergency rescue squad, which in Toney would have been the volunteer fire department. Ardmore Shopper headline: KICK THE CAN GAME GONE WRONG. FORTY-YEAR-OLD MALE RESCUED FROM A THREE-FOOT DRAINPIPE. Side Note: No one "Home free."

So in order to avoid the potential bad publicity and minimize physical damage, we took the sensible approach, totally opposite to what our ten- and eleven-year-old selves would have done, and mostly congregated at the back of the house or behind the old well house. We didn't even bother to split up, which of course made it easier for the cousin that was "it" to knock out three or four of us in a single swoop. All she had to do was peer around the corner, and while running, (lumbering is probably a better word), back to the front yard, call out our names and where we were located, set a foot on the can and "voila" half the players were captured. Unlike when we were kids, there were no signs of indignation, the stomping of feet or faces registering displeasure signaling the beginning of intense sulks. Instead, the captured cousins were content to return to the porch, sit down while rubbing aching joints and muscles, catch their breath and try to answer the questions that had always perplexed us like why Grandpa derived such pleasure from pinching the fire out of us with his toes or how was it possible that someone actually named a cousin Whistle-britches.

As for the cousins still in hiding or really just hanging out behind the old well house, all they had to do was split up and perform a sacrificial maneuver. When "it" called out the names and locations of those in one group who had made themselves easily visible by increasing the volume of their casual banter, the others bolted, (another misnomer considering our stamina), from the opposite side of the house and beat her to the can. One cousin kicked it with the last bit of energy left in a now throbbing foot while the rest yelled "Home free!"

We didn't know that this would be the last time we all gathered at our grandmother's house. Other aunts and uncles and even some of the cousins died, but distance, other obligations and in some cases illness prevented us from being together to mourn their passage. Phone calls, cards and flowers became the precedent. It was as if the joyous chorus of voices screaming "Home free" that night released us for good. Rather than scattering to hide, we left to resume lives that were much-removed from the farm set atop a hill on the north side of Dan Crutcher Road. Now that the farm has been sold, we can only revisit those nights of cousin-hood in our minds.

As I grow older, I have become a ready traveler back to those times. The scent of honeysuckle on a breeze, spotting a holly tree by the side of the road, hearing the shrieks of children playing in yards at sunset, and even placing what seems to be the perfect size can in the recycling bin can sometimes transport me. It helps that I miss the feeling of being unencumbered. When I feel especially trapped by things, people or circumstances, I wish for my escape to be as simple as the kicking of a can and the utterance of those magical words. There are times I can't stop myself. I take a deep breath, gaze into the darkness and offer up those words and all they represent to anyone who might hear, to the cousins who are alive and those that have passed, to the sky and the stars and to all those that, like me, feel cornered and need to be rescued. "Home free" spills off my tongue and through my lips. "Home free" jettisons from my mouth and parachutes into the night.

Mama

I am six years old and sitting in a first grade classroom. This is well before there are kindergartens or day-cares, so this is my first time to be away from home and my mother. My teacher is older and a bit rotund. She seems kind and I am a quick learner. I am in the bluebird reading group. I don't yet know what that means other than we only meet with the teacher once a day. The other bird groups sit with her in a circle at the front of the room several times a day. I wonder if my group is less likable. It is the first time I have met these kids. We all live in the rural area of Madison County. Our houses are nowhere close to each other. We don't have play dates or birthday parties with each other. The other kids I have known up to this time are my brothers and cousins. None of them are in my class. What should *be the simplest of decisions or choices seem overwhelming to me. I desperately need to pee. I finally have no choice but to approach the teacher who is with a group and ask to go to the bathroom. She tells me it is not time yet for the class to go and directs me back to my seat. I am squirming now, shifting my legs in a frantic motion. I am too frightened to ask again. It doesn't matter as I can feel the warm pee fill my underwear, soak my jeans and then after puddling in my seat start to drip with the sound of summer rainfall on the floor below. I don't understand options yet. So, I take what I think is my only recourse. I lay my head down on my desktop, and long before there is anything called Gorilla glue, bond myself to the wood, so no one can move me. I am oblivious to the time that passes. I hear other students' voices excitedly talking about my accident. I hear my teacher's voice and feel her stubby fingers attempting to pry my hands and arms away from the desk. I refuse to move. I have gained a super-human strength in my six-year-old arms that I think can only be gained with the first encounter with humiliation. It is not until I feel my mother's presence, her head lowered until it is next to mine, and hear her words of inquiry of what happened that I loosen my hold. And in an instant I am in her arms wrapped tightly around her with my head buried against her shoulder. She doesn't seem to care that I am so pee-soaked that it is now permeating the dress she is wearing. It is through muffled sobs and the material of her dress, since I refuse to move my face away so anyone else can see me, that I relate I had asked to go to the bathroom and the teacher told me I'd have to wait. Mama turned so quickly that the skirt of her dress created such air turbulence that papers flew off of kids' desks. The teacher's hair, though cut short and combed back in a severe fashion, seemed to rise from her scalp. Even pressed tightly against her shoulder, her words were so loud, I could hear them distinctly. "If my son ever again asks you permission to go to the bathroom and you say no, I promise you will regret it." After that there was total silence in the room. The teacher did not respond. The other kids were afraid to make a sound. The only noise was the swishing sound of Mama's skirt as she turned and then the click of the classroom door as it closed behind us.*

I don't know when my mother changed. And now I am even questioning if she really changed or if the meanness within her just became more magnified. Was it always there and I chose not to see it? Up until this time I have always thought that her stroke was the precipitating factor for the change. It was, after all, a catastrophic event in her life. She had been living independently up until that point. When my father died, she seemed to attack life with a vengeance as if she were a bird let out of a cage. She spent time at the local Senior Center, traveling with a local senior group and even volunteering at the elementary school where my brothers and I had gone many years ago. But, there were signs even then that I neglected to acknowledge. Sunday dinners that had always involved my brothers, their spouses, their children, an ever-changing group of friends and other relatives suddenly dissolved into a group of two, my mother and me. It was as if my father had been the main reason everyone came. And when he wasn't there anymore, everyone had better things to do. There were times like holidays when the family would return, but even those were tempered events when festivities were completed quickly so the participants could scatter like chipmunks running from a cat.

So, in some staged election of which I was either not aware or purposely kept in the dark, I became permanently "it." You can't tag anyone if their paths follow strangely circuitous routes that neither come close to your mother's house nor follow predictable patterns. Sunday would come, dinner would be served and Mother and I would sit at the table facing each other. What followed was her diatribe regarding everyone that was not there, how all their problems could be fixed, what their future problems were going to be, the down and outs at the Senior Center, the collapse of civilization in Ardmore since a band of midgets had moved in, how Fox news had pretty well predicted the downfall of our country, why I should be wary of anyone or everyone

I knew and in the end, as she packed what seemed like 40 Tupperware containers with food I would never eat, a question that seemed of such little import that it was often offered as a muffled aside, "How are you doing?"

Visits from that point on became testier and testier. Though I had always considered myself an adept conversationalist, I could not for the life of me alter the direction of a conversation. When she would begin an assault on someone who had the week before been a friend, I would inquire how her Braves were doing (she was a diehard Atlanta Braves fan). She would respond with a brief recount of how they were mismanaged, noting the players who were not playing their best and then resume her complaints about how her former friend had insisted on eating at a restaurant she personally hated. Maybe it was her favorite place, I would counter. A strange, sharp and dismissive burst of air would expel from her lungs. Maybe she wouldn't go back to the Senior Center anymore, as apparently all the other attendees that day had agreed with her now-former friend. Oh yeah, now the midget threat had decreased to a degree more commiserate with their size only to be replaced by gypsies. How she knew they were gypsies, I don't know. But they were there right in downtown Ardmore just waiting for unsuspecting senior citizens like my mother to let down their guard and be fleeced like the woolliest of sheep.

I am ten years old. I am excited. My older brothers are allowing me to play basketball with them on the court our dad made for us. It used to be a grassy area, but the grass has long been worn away by the trampling of our tennis shoes, leaving a fairly smooth and solid dirt circle. I don't know if I had ever paid attention before to the pole that holds up the rim and backboard. Today I see that it was once the trunk of a tree. The knots where limbs used to jut off from the trunk are still there. We are taking turns shooting the ball from all angles of the court. It is a good day for me as they are giving me shots equal to the number of theirs. They are encouraging me even though my shots are nowhere close to the accuracy of their own. There are so many sounds in the country that we don't hear her as she approaches. It isn't until we hear the sound of her voice that we realize she is there. Mother reaches for the ball from my oldest brother and tells us we are going to have to be tough to play on a basketball team. I remember that she has told us about the sports she played in high school. I am thrilled she is willing to teach us. First, she tells my oldest brother to try and guard her. She starts on the dirt court at the farthest point from the goal. She turns her back to my brother, juts her rear end out and begins dribbling the ball. Though my brother tries, there is no way that his arms can reach around to even get close to the ball. She moves backward toward the goal, driving my brother with her. As she approaches the goal, she forces her rear end out in a sudden jerking motion that knocks my brother against the post with the knobs. I see him wince in pain, but he doesn't make a sound. After she has banked her shot into the goal, she tells him he has to learn to stand his ground and not allow another player to push him around the court. Next, it is my middle brother's turn. He is more adept at the game than my oldest brother. So, when Mother begins the same maneuver she used before, he makes a motion around her to her right and as she turns to counter him, he quickly darts to the left and almost grabs the ball. With her right hand still busy dribbling the ball, She swings her left arm out and catches him on the side of his head with her elbow. He ends up on the dirt a good two yards from her. As he stands up, rubbing the side of his face, she tells him sometimes you have to foul to let your opponent know you mean business and if you have to foul make sure it counts. She casually fires the ball from mid court and it slips through the hoop. Finally, it is my turn. I am not sure I want to do this, but I know if I don't, my brothers might not ask me to play again. I take my position behind her. I am so small that my head barely reaches her rear end that has already been pushed into the menacing position. She only has to push back once to throw me off balance. My feet become tangled and I land hard on my back. She dribbles around my prone body and makes an easy layup. The lesson is over for the day. She tells us its time to start supper. None of us move until we hear the den door close behind her.

And then came the stroke. It was a simple procedure according to the doctor. Only a small blockage in an artery in her neck that needed to be cleared. All went well the doctor told my niece, a lady from the Center who was one of the few friends she had left that had come to sit with us, and me as we stood in the waiting area of the hospital. In a few minutes we would be able to see her. He returned fifteen minutes later with a grim look on his face. It seems they had missed a piece of the blockage which had dislodged and then traveled to a part of her brain causing damage. How much damage could not be assessed until later. Perhaps, it was her resilient nature, she was after all a strong woman and had always been a hard worker, or maybe it was the meanness within her that had grown like a dark force in a Harry Potter novel. Whatever the cause, she survived with minimal long-lasting impairment considering the severity of the stroke. Her speech was a little slurred for a bit, along with a drooping on the right side of her face, and there were some balance issues due to her right leg being a tad unsteady. But, the long-lasting and most life-changing result was the loss of the use of her right arm. If she had been left-handed like my dad, this wouldn't have been so critical, but she was right-handed, and suddenly facing a multitude of daunting tasks where either your dominant hand or both hands working in unison were required.

I would like to say at this point that the troops rallied, you know, fallen comrade and all. There was a brief flurry of activity since Mother opted out of rehab and opted in to the therapists coming to her home. I understood her strategy. She wanted them all to come to her and do their magic in her throne room. Her throne? A reclining lift chair that would always position her just right to both lament her limitations and emphasize her plans for everyone's life from now on. My middle brother and his wife did find a lady at their church who needed money and was willing to fill in the times that the therapists wouldn't be there. Bless her heart. She was a simple country girl trying to raise her daughter without the support of a husband. I don't remember how long she lasted, a month or two I think. It was just long enough for Mother to begin to think of her as her slave. She ate what Mother ate. She watched the TV shows that Mother liked. Everything else she seemed to do wrong or at least required Mother's discerning eye and constant directions on how it should have been done in the first place. I think what finally broke her was when Mother began thinking of things she needed her to do or pick up on her way to the house, like picking up a paper, a can of Vienna sausages, stamps from the post office, fresh tomatoes if she could find some, could she come a little earlier (she arrived at 6 am each day). "Oh yeah, can you stay later today when you get here? Buy some clippers, my toenails are getting a tad thick and long." One day the helper called my brother and said she couldn't do it anymore. No kidding. It's a wonder she didn't request waterboarding or shock therapy. She is probably still haunted by the sound of that chair's incessant hum as it raised my Mother up to cast her daily judgments and admonitions.

I am twelve years old. It is a sunny day and I am lost in a place where I am truly happy. Water, like the deep woods, always seems to calm me and excite me at the same time. I move in a thousand different directions. One minute I am playing Marco Polo in the middle of the pool. The next, I am involved in underwater tag which we are sure was invented right here at Blue Water Springs Park. There is so much happening that I am constantly shifting my attention to the shouts, the splashes, the bare feet running on the wet cement, the lifeguards' yells to slow down, and the diving boards as they bend and release. Still there are moments that I turn to check on her. I am not sure if I am checking to see if she is still there or simply hoping that she has seen me complete an intricate maneuver off the high diving board. When I look, she is still there sitting on the other side of the tall chain link fence that surrounds the pool. She is snapping beans from the two large brown paper bags she has brought with her. She is engaged in conversation with other mothers that have also brought their children to swim. I think, what can I do to get her attention? I stride around the pool and climb the ladder leading to the high diving board. I take two deep breaths as I visualize what I am about to do. I take four measured steps, launch myself from the end of the board and complete a successful one-and-a-half dive. When I push my head out of the water I look to where she is sitting. Her focus has not wavered from the bags of beans at her feet. It is not her attention that I am seeking. It is her approval. It will always be her approval.

Being "it" does not come with perks. What it brings is a never-ending series of obligations or expectations that vary only in the degree of angst and dread that fill my body and mind, often causing my breathing to become more labored and my heart rate to soar like a dying eagle. Thus it is as I pick my mother up to drive her to Thanksgiving dinner at my niece's house in middle Tennessee. At her house I can sometimes move away from the negativity if it becomes too unbearable. In a car for almost an hour, I have no place to escape. She catches me off guard with her words as we travel north. I am busy checking the speedometer. I have discovered that when driving her somewhere, or at times when leaving her house after a visit that I have a tendency to drive at break-neck speeds. Once I found myself going 90 miles per hour on Highway 53 after an especially contentious exchange. I had to pull off on a side road to allow my nerves to settle. So, on this day I am at first oblivious to her words. They are so often cutting and vinegary that I have begun to play songs in my head to drown most of them out. It is not until she repeats them that the words register in my brain. She is thinking it might be time to look at assisted living places. She had seen one in Fayetteville, Tennessee that she liked. It was nestled in woods and deer wander into the large yard of the facility at times. I told her it might be best for her. She could make friends there. It wouldn't be as difficult for her to complete all the daily tasks she now faces. I felt a strange sense of relief after that trip. I should have known better. Nothing is ever that simple with Mother. My middle brother went to visit the place. He told me it was indeed serene, clean and wonderful. He filled out all the necessary paperwork as they had an unexpected opening which was extremely rare due to increasing interest and requests from potential clients. And then suddenly like a summer thunderstorm descending on Ardmore all hell seemed to break loose. No, it wasn't the midgets. And apparently the gypsies had reached their fleecing quota and left the scene. Isn't it always the family members who aren't around for the daily demands that suddenly appear like the Lone Ranger and Tonto to save the innocent maiden from the train, or in this case my mother, the maiden in danger, with my middle brother and me the conductors railroading her into an assisted living home? The Ranger and Tonto were two of her grandchildren. And just as soon as they convinced her that her house was where she needed to stay, they became like a wind in the old west disappearing over the horizon and carrying two stray tumbleweeds with it. Hi Ho Silver, indeed.

The next phase of Mother's senior crusades began with serious verbal altercations between her and me, her and my middle brother, her and anyone else that would listen and then her and me once again. According to Mother, my middle brother had concocted the whole scheme to put her away against her will. And speaking of wills, she would remove him, a plausible punishment, if she had not done so at an earlier time. When I reminded her it was initially her idea, it suddenly became a conspiracy that he and I had plotted in some smoke-filled room, of course, where we had Mother's picture attached to a dart board. She, like a true southern matriarch, rose to the challenge. She somehow hoodwinked, and I do mean hoodwinked after reexamining the whole affair, the director of the Senior Center (and her friend at the time) to agree to spend three nights a week with her and do all the things she needed. Not to overload her too much, she also hired a housekeeper to come once or twice a month to complete the real grunt work. Her true coup, however, came from my uncle, my father's sister's husband. Somehow, they had remained diligent in their visits with her after my father died. My guess as to how this happened is my uncle's hearing was so bad that he rarely ever knew what Mother said. My aunt was so religious that she had a personal altar constructed off her bedroom. So, I'm sure after every visit her knees ended up raw or chaffed. Anyway, my uncle who had retired from Chrysler had a special knob that could be attached to the steering wheel of a car. It was designed for people who only had the use of one hand or arm. Hello. Can anyone spot the new danger that appeared on the radar in Ardmore? Yes, he installed one for her. Yes, she began driving with her left hand and a shaky right foot. She had shown my brother and me what she was capable of doing. You would think the meanness would abate. You would think she would be happy. You would be wrong on both counts.

I am fourteen years old. I have made a foolish blunder. The World Series has started and all the boys in our PE class are placing bets. I know little about baseball and even less about the teams playing. Still, in order to fit in, I bet fifty cents with another boy in the class. My team loses. He wants his money. I put him off for days as it is the only money my parents give me each day. I use it to buy the two milks I am supposed to drink as part of a regimen to cure the ulcers in my stomach. The ulcers were diagnosed when I began to throw up almost daily. According to the doctor, he had never seen such a bad case in someone so young. My parents never seemed to question what could be making me so nervous, or with the severity of the symptoms, a nervous wreck. Today is my day of reckoning. He has told me if I don't bring the money, he will beat it out of me. I have never been in a fight. One would think being raised with older brothers, a fight would have been inevitable, but I have learned early that a simple yell for Mother always halted my brothers' physical assaults. In other situations when confronted I have always been able to use words to escape. Today, words will not save me. So, when PE class ends and we walk into the locker room to change, there are already shooting pains in my stomach. He is waiting inside the door. Before I can even offer the money, he knocks me to the floor and straddles my chest. Just as he is about to hit me with a clinched fist, two boys in my class pull him off me.

They tell him I have a broken finger and wait till it heals, so it will be a fair fight. I do have a broken finger. It is encased in a metal splint. It had happened when I was playing football with my older brothers and their friends. He tells me he still wants his money, but turns and crosses the locker room to change clothes for class. I am so shaky, I can barely button up my shirt. The rest of the day is a blur for me. I make eye contact with no one. I am sure every muffled conversation is about me. There are times when I am sure the nausea will overtake me, but I hold on until the end of the school day. Fortunately for me, I don't have to ride the bus. My mother is working at the school now and waits for me in the teacher's parking lot. I almost make it to the car before I begin throwing up. It is so frequent and forceful that I can barely catch my breath. When it finally subsides, I am too weak to tell her anything else but the truth. It isn't until two days later that I return to school. I immediately seek out the boy and give him the fifty cents. I will do without milk for one day. He takes the money, but never looks at me directly. It is not until later in the day between classes that I find out the reason. The boy's sister comes to me and tells me how sorry she is that I am sick and that her brother made it worse. She tells me not to worry. My mother has talked to him and told him to never bother me again. I should be relieved. I am not. All I feel is humiliation and a sudden churning in my stomach.

What ensued for a couple of years is what I will call Mother's gold plated reign in Ardmore. She became so self-absorbed that everyone was expected to bow to her every wish and whim. Woe to those who did not. Had it been allowed and not resulted in a prison sentence for her, she would have had their heads removed and placed on the top of tall spiked poles beside the downtown streets. There were so many it would have rivaled the Christmas decorations the city used to adorn their light poles each year. What she was allowed to do was produce a long detailed rant about what was wrong with them and then with that strange exhale of breath thing she did along with a sound that is hard to spell, but something close to "gah," exclude them forever from her life. It was almost like that kid in one of the episodes of the *Twilight Zone* who could wish people into a horrifying world inside the TV. I don't know where Mother wished hers, but they were no longer part of her world. My brother and I always pictured those exiled as doing happy dances, taking their first good deep breaths in years and sleeping with contented smiles of relief on their faces.

She drove everywhere she needed to go in Ardmore using her left hand on that knob on the steering wheel. There were limitations as she had to park where she could always pull forward to exit. She never mastered backing up because it was difficult for her to shift her body with the right side never fully recovering from the stroke. Where were the Ardmore police for heaven's sake? But, she was somehow able to complete her daily tasks like going to the bank, the post office, the grocery store and most importantly the Senior Center every day it was open. If her destination was outside the city of Ardmore, she always had her paid caretaker, the Senior Center director, to take her. And take her she did, all according to Mother's schedule, not her own. Woe be to her if she had a conflicting family obligation or center business that required her presence. They would simply have to be changed or Mother would sulk and complain, remind her of the money she was paying her and perhaps even paint a picture using words of what her head would look like on a spike.

As for me, it became a horrendously oppressive period of time. In addition to my customary obligation to be at her house every Sunday for dinner, I acquired a never-ending and seemingly increasing set of duties. Since her right hand no longer functioned, I had to write out the checks to pay her bills. This also included balancing her checkbooks. Although that sounds minor, the fact that she had been a bookkeeper with the school system before she retired made it an ominous task. She would scour her checkbooks after I left like a hungry bird looking for a worm. Any mistake she found would lead to a lecture on the best way to do it or in reality the way she would do it. In addition, there were always things she wanted done in the house. If I questioned why her caretaker or housekeeper didn't do these things, she always answered they wouldn't be there until tomorrow. The bottom line was she wanted things done when she wanted them done. I wasn't worried about the spike. I didn't want to hear that now chilling "gah" sound or experience her talent of crying without producing tears and the reminder that she only had the use of one hand. And truly the worst part about it was that I had to be there longer. Maybe, that was her true intention after all. It gave her more time to fill me in on every negative thing that had happened, every misdeed she had witnessed, every instance when someone had misspoken and how in the end she was always right. Most of it involved the Senior Center where she spent the majority of her time. Nothing was too innocuous to share. Someone had cheated at Rook or dominoes. She could have won four Rook games if her partner hadn't been so stupid to play the wrong cards at the most critical times. So-and-so had lost a piece of the jigsaw puzzle that was almost finished. Someone who never brought anything in had taken more than their fair share of the free vegetables a local farmer had dropped off. The ones that were her friends, meaning that they always agreed with her or did exactly as she asked, were given reprieves. Either their brains were becoming more and more addled or their children were ungrateful and causing them too much grief for them to think straight. The ones that weren't her friends were the hapless ones who had made the mistake of disagreeing with her or simply stating an honest opinion. They were never aware that she had done one of three things, pointed them out as wealthy and easy prey to the gypsies, was having another spiked pole erected on the square or was, as she sat there appearing quite angelic, wishing them into the TV on the wall, the one she wouldn't allow to be played because the sound interfered with her regular announcement that she was shooting the moon in a Rook game. I heard it all before I would load the Tupperware containers of what had become mostly inedible food into my car, throw gravel with my quickly accelerating wheels as I backed out and then shoot south to Huntsville like the Saturn 5 trying to escape the Earth's gravitational pull.

It is a beautiful day with a clear blue sky and almost no clouds. There is a slight breeze that seems to deflect much of the summer heat. I am sixteen years old and I am wishing that all days could be like this. The whole family is at the house, both brothers along with a couple of cousins. We are doing what we enjoy most, playing games outside. Today the game is croquet. My oldest brother has set up a very tricky course, wickets on the edge of ditches, behind grassy mounds, and even teetering on high knolls. We play as teams with the object being for all members of a team to finish the course first to win. There is also an added incentive for the player first out. They become "the rover" and get to continue to play with the sole purpose of raising havoc for the opposing team. I am happy not to be on my mother's team. She may appear to be a team player only to go rogue during the game serving her own amusement and hampering the play of her teammates. We are playing at a fairly quick pace. I am pleased with myself. I am hitting my ball solidly. I am always a good team player. I sometimes choose not to proceed through a wicket in order to provide a teammate the chance to ricochet off my ball and move ahead of me. If my ball lands against an opponent's ball I will drive their ball as allowed by the rules of the game. Today, I am more about strategy than aggression. So, I drive them into areas that give them the least chance of making it through the next wicket. There is lots of laughter today. Everyone is in a good mood whether it be the weather, playing the game or simply being all together again. As the game progresses, it is clear my oldest brother will be "the rover." It is a coup for our team. He becomes quite scrappy hindering the progress of our opponents. I watch him drive their balls right and left. And finally there are only three players left, my mother, my oldest brother and me. Both my mother and I are through the last wicket. My oldest brother's ball had been driven by the last finishing opponent to a spot too far away to help me. Mother's shot is perfect. Her ball ends up sitting directly in front of the double wickets with a straight shot to the pole and victory for her team. Our only chance is for me to hit her ball and knock it out of position. I miss her completely and land about a foot beyond her ball. When she steps up to her ball, mallet in hand, it looks like she is going to take the easy win for her team. Instead, she turns and knocks her ball to nestle up against mine. No one speaks although her teammates are shaking their heads in disbelief. She places her foot on the top of her ball to anchor it and then drives my ball with such force that it rolls completely out of the yard, across the road and into a ditch on the other side. By this time my oldest brother is able to get close enough to hamper her from hitting the pole. He keeps her busy while I eventually make it into the yard and then finally hit the pole to seal our team's win. Her team is furious with her, but she seems oblivious. When I ask her why she slammed me rather than going for a victory for her team, She shrugs her shoulders and laughs. "Sometimes, it's not about winning, son." Her words are beyond my understanding at sixteen. But, I look at her differently at that moment. I feel a strange disconnection and a strong desire not to be like her.

Like all monarchies, it is usually someone close that is responsible for the ruler's downfall. In Mother's case it was her caretaker, the director of the Senior Center and her best friend at the time. It was hard to piece together what really did occur. According to Mother her friend raised her voice and yelled at her, something no senior citizen should be forced to endure. According to the accused, her friend, Mother would not let something go until she, the accused, had to firmly disagree with her. If I were looking at all the facts, and also weighing all the encounters I have had with Mother, my guess would be her friend finally cracked. You listen to the tirades, the releases of breath followed by the wicked "gahs" and feel the negativity hit you in the face like a gust of the most humid hot air you have ever experienced until you snap. There was no reasoning with mother. She was never one to forgive. She had never forgiven her youngest sister for we still don't know what and hasn't spoken to her for almost ten years. As a result of the verbal altercation at the Senior Center, she lost her most faithful companion, her driver for all doctor's appointments and shopping trips and heaven help her, her ally in all disputes that arose on almost a daily basis at the Senior Center. One would think this might have tempered her negativity as she needed help from others, but it did nothing of the sort. She became angrier and that probably led to her final hurrah as a force in the Ardmore community.

With no one else available or willing to take her on, the housekeeper, who could never even vacuum to Mother's satisfaction, was promoted to driver. It was on one of her infamous shopping trips with her new minion, when she typically bought enough clothes for herself to almost create a completely new wardrobe, that she took her life-changing fall. Even as they wheeled her out on the gurney, and in intense pain, I'm sure she was able to grab red dot sale articles of clothing. It was after all Senior Day with an additional 20% off of all sale items. How could she resist? The resulting broken shoulder took her through a lengthy hospital stay, a stint in rehab in an extremely depressing nursing home that she chose because it was in Ardmore, and then to the assisted living facility where she now lives. I know it was a traumatic time for her. How could I not? She reminded me every day. For my middle brother and me, it was as if we were living in hell. The logistics of finding a suitable place for her, clearing out and boxing a lifetime of accumulated things that belonged to someone who never threw anything away while continuing to buy at an increasingly unbelievable rate, and at the same time maintaining a suitable visitation schedule probably aged us both by a good ten years. If that were not enough, our oldest brother who was an alcoholic and never any help was found dead in his trailer just north of Pulaski, Tennessee. She had never placed any demands on him. Even though he had almost destroyed our dad and her financially and emotionally, all she asked of him was a daily call when he sounded sober. All she said of his death when we told her was that she had done everything she could do for him.

It is a very nice place where she lives. My brother painstakingly brought all the furniture we thought she truly loved and created a comfortable living area. He even managed to include a huge display cabinet that houses her prized Fenton glass collection. Her oldest niece who is an interior decorator came to hang the designer curtains and arrange the pictures on the wall. It was not enough. Nothing was ever enough. For the first few months that she was there, she was sullen and morose. She complained about the food, the other residents, the people that worked there, the fact that I had sold her car (the doctor said she should never have been driving in the first place), that she was too far away from her friends at the Senior Center (if there were any, they never came to visit nor called), that all her stuff was gone (it had all been boxed and stored at my brother's warehouse), and finally, that she had been brought there to die. I heard all of this and more each time I visited until one day I snapped like her old friend did. I'm sure my voice was as high as my blood pressure at the time. I told her if all she was going to do is complain, then I might as well go. As I left her room she was yelling that my brother and I had destroyed her life and had taken everything she loved away. When the door closed behind me, I didn't plan on going back.

As I drive home from the Space and Rocket Center where I work part time as a tour guide, my head is filled with possibilities. I am twenty-one years old and about to graduate from UAH. I have found my true self there, I think, in a group of people who are eclectic, smart and most importantly accepting of all my idiosyncrasies. I have made the Dean's list again and am smiling from the knowledge that my mother will be pleased. I have lived with my parents for the past two years while I worked and finished my degree. It has not always been easy as my mother's rules are often the opposite of my father's, but today, I am sure all past contentions with her will be eased. All is good. When I pull into the driveway, she is sitting in a chair on the back patio. When I open the door of my car, she is already up and marching toward me. The look on her face is one I have seen many times while growing up. Most often it appeared when she was fighting with my father. Sometimes it appeared when she was infuriated by something one of my brothers or I had done. It contained so much anger she couldn't maintain a single position of her mouth. I don't even have the opportunity to review in my head what I could have possibly done wrong before her rant begins. "After all we've done for you, I'd think you would have at least a little respect for your dad and me. Instead, you choose to bring something into our house that would get not only you in serious trouble, but us as well. We could lose this house. We could lose everything we own. And apparently you don't care." I have no idea what she is talking about until she holds out a plastic sandwich baggie that is filled with something green and leafy. "When I was putting clothes away in one of your dresser drawers, this is what I found." I am immediately relieved as I know what it is and would have laughed except I know she would knock me to the ground if I did. "Mother, it's rabbit tobacco I picked with Grandma last weekend." "I'm not stupid," she countered. It was not only the set of her mouth she didn't control now, but also her body. She is so angry she is shaking. I would have gotten back in my car and driven away had my middle brother not arrived at that point. I quickly told him what was happening. He took the bag from Mother's hand, opened it and smelled. He looked at our mother. "It really is only rabbit tobacco." Mother was never one to apologize or even admit when she was wrong. She turned and went inside the house. I decide not to mention the Dean's list. What's the use. I realize it will never be enough. Soon, I will be gone. I am not totally innocent. My real stash is under the front seat of my car.

Of course, I went back. As she has been there over a year now, some things have changed. It is more rare that she laments being there. That is not to say she is entirely happy about it. But, her physical limitations are increasing in number and magnitude. She will deny she needs help, but requires it more and more the older she gets. So, when things become tense between us as they always do and will from time to time, she doesn't hit me with how I destroyed her life. It is now how I wish her dead. It is her new rebuttal if I disagree with her or share personal plans that involve my being away from her for any period of time. She has also found a way to reclaim her throne. She now rules her assisted living cottage and will, if she has time left, take control of the other two cottages in the compound as well. She accomplished it in her typical fashion charming the people in charge until they let their guards down and then moving in for the control jugular. She has intimidated all the other residents that are weak, and the ones that aren't she has worked to get them moved out. Already, two are gone and there are two more on her radar. My brother and I are in set routines as far as visitation goes. He goes only on Wednesdays and it is mandatory for him that his daughter and grandson are there for the majority of the visit. I understand this completely as his and Mother's relationship has always been extremely contentious. It is a strange thing that she was able to forgive our oldest brother for his multitude of transgressions and yet cannot do the same for her middle son. Maybe, he reminds her too much of our father. It is a hard one to call, but still, he somehow keeps his weekly visit. As for me, it is usually once during the week to bring her cash and various items she requests. Since, I have no one to come with me and help deflect her negativity, I try to time it to about 40 minutes before her lunchtime. I spend more time watching the clock on the side table beside her chair than I do looking at her. Even then what I hear is often too much for me to bear. Someone in the next cottage is cheating at Bingo. She suspects one lady's son is duplicating the Bingo bucks (counterfeit Bingo bucks, oh my) that they win in their Bingo games and use once a week to bid for things at the Bingo store. This means she can outbid Mother on things she really wants, like a pack of tissues or bag of Doritos. One lady is smelly again and must be sleeping in urine-soaked clothes. One man's pants are too small and when he sits you can see his butt crack. One lady purposely backed her walker over Mother's toe. Someone keeps turning the porch fans off while Mother and her friends are sitting on the porch. The food is either overcooked or undercooked. It is never seasoned correctly. There is never enough. Something they cooked ran straight through her. Her pills were five minutes late. Her pills were 10 minutes early. I hear a variation of these complaints every time I visit. They always follow one of two intros, "You know I am not one to complain and I never ask them do anything for me," or "I am one of a few residents who still has a sound mind and it drives me crazy how the others will repeat themselves, over and over again." Really?

This classroom is much different than my first one. It is paneled and has no windows. My other one had floor-to-ceiling windows that covered one whole wall. There were even cantilevered windows at the bottom that swung out to allow in fresh air on temperate weather days. I am wondering if at thirty-six I am capable of such a swing in my professional life. Is the windowless room somehow portentous of how I will fare teaching elementary kids with special needs? The special needs part doesn't bother me. I spent ten years of my life teaching severely and profoundly retarded adults before completing my master's degree so that I could work in a public school system. As I rifle through the scant resources in my new classroom, I reflect on my first day at the other school. When the director walked me into my room, she offered that I would have two permanent aides to assist me, and I would also have two aides each day from the cottages where the students lived. They would always be male, she interjected. I should have asked her why, but didn't. Thirty minutes into my first day, I knew why. The largest of my students jumped up from his table, grabbed a smaller female and sank his teeth into her shoulder. She screamed which made two other students start to hit themselves with their fists. An older student wearing a helmet that prevented damage to her head when she fell tried to intervene and in so doing did a double rolling flip across the floor. While every staff member was attempting to deal with the students involved in the melee, a smaller albino student opened one of the windows, dropped through and raced away from the school. I no longer questioned the rationality of staff assignments in my classroom.

Oddly enough, as my attention is drawn back to this dark room that will soon be filled with a much younger and hopefully less volatile group of students, I think of my mother. She is the reason I have this job. I had already been promised a position at a high school in the city. The principal was more impressed with my ability to wrestle and maintain control of unpredictable adult students than my academic background. It was just a matter of signing the paperwork. When my mother found out that the county school system in which she worked had not offered me a job, she marched into the central office and pretty much threw her weight around. Voila! A job suddenly became available at one of the elementary schools. There was no interview when I went to the school. I was simply shown to my new classroom. I am relieved that I am not going to be at the city high school and excited about working with younger students. I am somewhat embarrassed by my mother's intercession and wondering what price I will have to pay. With Mother, there is always a quid pro quo.

In addition to the middle of week visit, I never lost the obligation to have lunch with her on Sunday. If I am lucky, and I use that word dubiously, I pick up food to take there and eat with her. If I am not, and this usually follows the whiniest voices she can muster espousing how she hasn't been out all week and has to get out of there even if for just a while, I pick her up to go out. Most of the time is consumed by her getting in and out of my car. It is a laborious process. It is not like watching something in slow motion. It is slow motion. It takes forever for her to bend down to get in and forever for her to establish her balance to get out. In both procedures her knees produce loud noises much like the snap, crackle and pop sounds Rice Krispies cereal makes when milk is poured over it. The same happens in the restaurant when she is getting in or out of a booth. And in my head I am always wondering if this is the time she won't be able to get up again. We are limited in the restaurants we can choose from. She doesn't like Mexican food, Italian and in no way Chinese. I once tricked her into a Greek place. She ate two bites off her plate. I loved it there. As we left, she told me this place wasn't a good idea. So, it is either City Cafe, where it takes 30 minutes for me to decipher her order to the waitress, or Gibson's where she always orders a plate of ribs that covers over half the table followed by a slab of pie to take with her. You would think that conversations in a busy restaurant would be easier. You would be wrong. Not only are they as caustic, but she has now begun to produce a cartoon character voice to mimic her new nemesis at the cottage, a red headed resident who is very sweet, but has diminished mental capacity. Somehow, this lady has come to believe she is part of the staff and must step in when she thinks someone needs help or is doing wrong. Nobody has told her that Mother already has taken over that job, so Mother is now constantly relaying to me every misstep the lady makes during the week and when she comes to the things she says, due to Mother's diminished hearing, she uses the cartoon voice so loudly that people two tables away can hear her. You got it. I am having lunch with Snidely Whiplash.

At this point in the ever-changing saga, Mother has a service she can call at any time to carry her anywhere she wants to go. This gives her the independence she accused us of taking away. Once she had them take her back to the Senior Center in Ardmore for a visit. It wasn't like she remembered. Actually, she didn't receive a royal welcome. She has no plans to go back. She always has cash to go shopping or to order in food when she thinks a meal is too crappy. My niece has three walk-in closets full of Mother's clothes, purses and shoes at her house. She regularly rotates them out in the closet in Mother's room. She could go a good four months or more and never wear the same thing. The cottage has a van that will take her anywhere on each Tuesday and Thursday. There is a Senior Center three miles from the cottage. Mother refuses to go. She says she played there in a Rook tournament once and the people there were shysters. She has ventured to one of the other cottages to play Bingo. She won't go to the third even though there is a gentleman who lives there and comes over when she asks him to help her with especially difficult jigsaw puzzles. Now she won't start another puzzle because she is sure someone like an undercover, dead-of-night, clandestine puzzle thief will take one of the pieces the instant before she has finished it. Or her last theory involves the redheaded resident who now not only wants to usurp her authority, but also wants to get under her skin by pocketing the last piece of the puzzle. Before her reign is over, she will rule them all. Even then she will not be content. She'll branch out to other assisted living facilities in the city and maybe beyond. She will need colonies, lots and lots of colonies. And their official flag will be embossed with an image of Mother and underneath it will be printed the word "gah."

I am sixty-one years old. Next month I will be sixty-two. I have retired from teaching. It remains to be seen whether this is a good decision or not. I am thinking not at this very minute as I am sitting in the blue wingback chair and separated by a side table from my mother in her lift chair. The wingback chair was originally gold. It may have been reupholstered other times before the blue, but it is the gold I remember. In my memory, it sits in the living rooms of every house where we lived. We were never instructed not to sit in it, we just didn't. It was formal and really for guests, and my brothers and I were never the formal types. My mind is wandering as it often does during our visits. It is a trick I have learned to employ to deflect the negative and most often ugly things she has to say. I used to tune in when she asked me a question, but after countless times when she would override my voice to answer the question herself, I knew she didn't really wish to hear what I had to say. As I am sitting here, I note that if the light from the window is just right, I can see my reflection in the glass front of the display case on the other side of her chair. It looks as if my face is next to hers. The older I get my features seem to favor hers more than my dad's. It is disturbing and I have to look away at anything else in the room that holds no truths. As she continues to talk, I am thinking of the realizations about her that have evolved in the past years. She will never be happy. She wasn't happy living alone in Ardmore. She wasn't happy when my dad was still alive. And though it makes my stomach churn to think it, I don't think she was truly happy when my brothers and I were young and life was fresh and new. I try to counter these feelings with images that appear in my head from time to time, her modeling one of the dresses she had made for herself, her face in the crowd at a ballgame where one of us had done well, her laughter when sitting with her sisters on grandma's porch and especially in the years later when she had begun to play softball and basketball again. Now, even those are overshadowed by the multitude of memories that register her discontent. I am still not sure when the anger and meanness came to be such a part of her or if it didn't either come with the unhappiness or perhaps cause it to some degree. People who have known her as long as I have tell me it was always there and I just didn't choose to see it. She was always my protector even when I should have been learning to protect myself. A friend of mine told me that people who are angry are covering their fears. I know Mother's current fears. She is afraid that her legs will give out and she'll have to use a wheel chair. She is afraid that her friends in the cottage will die and leave her alone. She is frightened of getting any older and I guess her inevitable death. These are fears I try to alleviate for her, but she is stubborn as always, and no matter what I say or do, it changes nothing. Still, there must be fears she has carried all of her life. If I could ever determine what they are or were, I would do my best to step in and face them for her as she did all those years ago for me in my first grade classroom. I look at the clock on the table beside her. It is her lunchtime. As I stand, I tell her I need to go and let her get to the dining room on time. I hear the whir of her chair as it lifts her up to stand. I hug her neck as she thanks me for coming. She follows me out the door and stands on the sidewalk, so that I can see her wave as I pull out of the parking lot to drive away. I can see her diminutive figure grow even smaller in my rearview mirror. I remind myself of the belief I have always held to be true regarding how our parents mold us. However you are raised or treated growing up, when you become an adult it is always your choice as to who you end up being or who you wish to become. If you can't handle the damage that was done to you all alone, you can always look for help from others. I know that I'm damaged in some ways, but I like who I am. As I turn onto the highway heading home, for once, I am not speeding. I take an inordinate amount of air into my lungs and release it slowly. "I like who I am," I voice to the other motorists on the road.

Acknowledgements

I wish to thank my friends, Barbara Arends, Merry Gaylor, Halley Hall and Pat Pope who graciously read or listened to my stories and offered suggestions and encouragement. In addition, I am grateful for Jennie Mitchell's ability to make my craziest text and notions appear good in print and for a most exceptional book cover. And perhaps most paramount, I must offer heartfelt thanks to my dear friend, Rosie Little. Without her exceptional editing skills, ideas, encouragement and willingness to listen to me on countless nights with sometimes too many glasses of wine on her back porch, this collection of stories would have never happened.

Made in the USA
Columbia, SC
04 June 2018